Longarm coul~~d~~ might lead him to the murderers...

He stopped for a moment and fished a cheroot out of his pocket, found a match and thumbed a fire, and bent his head to the small flame cupped inside the protective curl of his hands.

Far off to the left, somewhere beyond the railroad tracks, there was a wink of flame. Longarm only saw its spearpoint of fire out of the corner of his eye.

"Jesus!"

Longarm dropped flat against the ground, and the ugly *thupp* of a bullet whizzed past his ears...

Also in the LONGARM series
from Jove

LONGARM
LONGARM AND THE DRAGON
   HUNTERS
LONGARM AND THE RURALES
LONGARM ON THE HUMBOLDT
LONGARM IN NORTHFIELD
LONGARM AND THE GOLDEN LADY
LONGARM AND THE BOOT HILLERS
LONGARM AND THE BLUE NORTHER
LONGARM ON THE SANTA FE
LONGARM AND THE STALKING
   CORPSE
LONGARM AND THE COMANCHEROS
LONGARM AND THE DEVIL'S
   RAILROAD
LONGARM IN SILVER CITY
LONGARM ON THE BARBARY COAST
LONGARM AND THE MOONSHINERS
LONGARM IN YUMA
LONGARM IN BOULDER CANYON
LONGARM IN DEADWOOD
LONGARM AND THE GREAT TRAIN
   ROBBERY
LONGARM AND THE LONE STAR
   LEGEND
LONGARM IN THE BADLANDS
LONGARM IN THE BIG THICKET
LONGARM AND THE EASTERN DUDES
LONGARM IN THE BIG BEND
LONGARM AND THE SNAKE DANCERS
LONGARM ON THE GREAT DIVIDE

LONGARM AND THE BUCKSKIN
   ROGUE
LONGARM AND THE CALICO KID
LONGARM AND THE FRENCH ACTRESS
LONGARM AND THE OUTLAW
   LAWMAN
LONGARM AND THE LONE STAR
   VENGEANCE
LONGARM AND THE BOUNTY
   HUNTERS
LONGARM IN NO MAN'S LAND
LONGARM AND THE BIG OUTFIT
LONGARM AND SANTA ANNA'S GOLD
LONGARM AND THE CUSTER COUNTY
   WAR
LONGARM IN VIRGINIA CITY
LONGARM AND THE LONE STAR
   BOUNTY
LONGARM AND THE JAMES COUNTY
   WAR
LONGARM AND THE CATTLE BARON
LONGARM AND THE STEER
   SWINDLERS
LONGARM AND THE HANGMAN'S
   NOOSE
LONGARM AND THE OMAHA
   TINHORNS
LONGARM AND THE DESERT DUCHESS
LONGARM ON THE PAINTED DESERT
LONGARM ON THE OGALLALA TRAIL

TABOR EVANS

LONGARM

ON THE ARKANSAS DIVIDE

A JOVE BOOK

LONGARM ON THE ARKANSAS DIVIDE

A Jove Book/published by arrangement with
the author

PRINTING HISTORY
Jove edition/November 1984

ISBN: 0-515-07915-4

Jove books are published by The Berkley Publishing Group,
200 Madison Avenue, New York, N.Y. 10016. The words
"A JOVE BOOK" and the "J" with sunburst are trademarks
belonging to Jove Publications, Inc.

PRINTED IN THE UNITED STATES OF AMERICA

Chapter 1

"Lord God A'mighty!" Billy Vail blurted. His already pink-complected face reddened with a dark flush of what might have been embarrassment because it was not his habit to be blasphemous, particularly at five minutes until eight on a workday morning. He looked like he was about to utter an apology, but he did not. It was not his habit, either, to give apologies to his employees, especially for such minor lapses of character. Instead he completed the interrupted business of hanging his hat on its accustomed peg in his office.

Normally a controlled, even a proper, man, the United States Marshal for the Denver District, Department of Justice, Vail now seemed quite shaken by what confronted him in his own office. "What are *you* doing here?" he demanded.

The answer he received was hardly informative. "You have some lint on top of your head, Billy. Right in the middle of your bald spot. There. That's better."

Vail ran a hand unnecessarily again over the top of his pate, looked at it with suspicion as if to assure himself that the unexpected visitor had been having fun at the marshal's expense, then shook his head absently and took a seat behind the uncluttered expanse of his desk top.

Vail stared hard at the lean, brown man who had been waiting in the office before the marshal's arrival.

The man who faced him was tall, with wide shoulders and a horseman's narrow hips. He was a study in shades of brown, from his chestnut hair and sweeping chestnut moustache to the tanned and sun-wrinkled skin to the chocolate and brown hues of his pegged trousers, leather vest, and tweed coat. A snuff-brown Stetson lay on the floor beside the chair where the man was now lounging. His unbuttoned coat gapped open at the front of his lean belly, exposing the walnut-brown butt of a large-caliber revolver carried forward of his left hip and canted for a cross-body draw. A slender gold watch chain crossed fashionably from one vest pocket to the other. Vail knew that at one end of that chain would be the expected watch, but at the other there was clipped a small but lethal derringer pistol. Except for that spot of gold across his vest, the only other relief from the browns of the tall man was the white of his teeth when he gave the marshal an insolent and somewhat taunting grin and his keen gunmetal-blue eyes.

Vail knew the intruder quite well. He was Custis Long, the United States Marshal's best deputy. Well, best for field work; considerably less than that when it came to administrative chores.

Marshal Vail was beginning to recover from his surprise. "I asked what the hell you're doing here, Longarm?" Vail's surprise, almost to the point of shock, was caused by Deputy Long's long-established habit of reporting for work considerably after the usual appointed hour. To have the man show up in the office in advance of the start of the working day was virtually unheard of.

Long, commonly known to his friends and not a few of his enemies as Longarm, shrugged and shifted in his chair, pulling a lengthy and wickedly black cheroot from an inside coat pocket. He took his time about nipping off the tip and lighting it with a match that he dredged from another pocket.

"Well?" Vail demanded.

Longarm looked pained. "Damn it, Billy, I'm bored."

It was Vail's turn to grin. The pink-cheeked marshal, whose innocuous appearance had led many a wanted felon to false conclusions about Vail's abilities in a fight back when he had been a field man himself, looked positively pleased with this unexpected turn of events. There were times, more than a few of them, when Marshal Vail regarded Deputy Long as a personal cross he was required to bear. Now it seemed that the deputy was in search of a favor.

"You have been performing an invaluable service for your country, Deputy," Vail said happily.

"Balls," Longarm mumbled.

"What?" Vail was smiling with great good cheer now.

"I said 'balls,' Billy. Damn it, man, you've had me squiring that silly bastard of a congressman and his family for a solid week now." Longarm gave his boss a big-eyed look of sheer misery. "I swear, Billy, that man doesn't have the sense God gave your average pissant. And his wife is worse. She don't care what we're seeing, just who is seeing them do the seeing. Why, if there isn't some society writer handy to mark down every word the congressman speaks, that poor thing is turning her head and like to breaking her neck looking for a reporter."

"There are compensations," Vail said smugly. "I am told

the congressman has a daughter."

Longarm rolled his eyes heavenward. "She's the worst part of it all, Billy. The girl is fat and . . ."

"Plump, perhaps," Vail corrected. "Congressmen's daughters are not fat. They are plump."

"Fat, plump—damn it Billy, she's a walking suet ball. It's a wonder birds don't attack her on the streets. And those eyes, Billy. She keeps making moon eyes at me. Makes me think of a calf that's been grazing loco weed or something. It's awful. And I'm *bored*. Bored to the point of being near loco myself, Billy. So I come here this morning to ask you nice and polite to *please* give me some proper work to do."

Vail pursed his lips and pretended to give the request some thought. "I really don't think I can spare you right now, Longarm. Aside from the fact that the congressman and his family are so appreciative of your services—he was telling me that just the other day, by the way—there is the trial to consider. You might be required to testify again." Vail shook his head in mock sadness. "No, Longarm, you might be needed here in Denver. We wouldn't want to chance a mistrial, you know."

"Damn it, Billy, do you want me to beg? I'm begging. Well, almost. Besides, you know as well as I do that I've already given my testimony. They won't need me again."

"Defense counsel is making every effort to delay and obfuscate, Custis. They could call you back if they wanted. It would be entirely legal. If you weren't there to answer their questions . . . pfftt . . . mistrial." The marshal shook his head again. "Can't risk that, Longarm. We really can't."

"What if they wouldn't, Billy? What if we knew for sure that I won't have to testify again?"

"Oh, that might be different, Longarm. Possibly. I mean, I suppose the gentleman from Vermont might be able to get

4

along without your services. In the interests of duty and all that. But really, Custis, the Watson trial has been hanging on for two weeks now. Very technical stuff going on in the courtroom, the way I hear it. It's simply too risky to have you out on assignment if they should need you back on the stand again."

Longarm's expression softened. It was almost as if he were about to smile, but Vail could not tell that for sure, because the tall deputy suddenly began to cough and quickly raised a fist in front of his face.

"Are you all right, Longarm?"

The coughing stopped a the deputy took another pull on his cheroot. "Passing fair, Billy." This time he did smile. "Maybe better'n fair, in fact."

"Really?"

Longarm grinned at his boss. "I stopped in and had a word with the deputy U. S. attorney last night."

"Oh?"

"He said defense rested its case yesterday afternoon, late. All they got left is the closing arguments today and then it goes to the jury, Billy. There's no chance in hell I could be called back now."

Vail acted like he did not know whether to be pleased with that piece of information or disappointed because Long had so obviously succeeded in setting him up.

Both men, though, were looking forward to the conclusion of the trial that had been taking place in the federal courtroom. Chester Anthony Watson was a high-born and wealthy member of a high-born and wealthy family from the Northeast. He also happened to be completely amoral and had come west with the apparent intention of indulging himself. His tastes ran the gamut from simple, if vicious, battery through rape, sodomy, and murder. The legal excellence that affluence can provide had already allowed him to walk freely away from at least three and probably five serious crimes, including at least two murders. His mistake had been the brutalization and murder of a female land-office employee. That had been a federal offense, and Longarm had lost no time in bringing him in for trial. Now it looked like his expert counsel had run out of delaying tactics. Evidence supplied to the jury by Longarm in the early stages of the lengthy trial should surely now send Watson to the gallows.

"You're sure of that, Longarm?"

"Billy." Longarm sounded reproachful. "Would I lie to you?" He grinned and added, "About anything that could be checked up on so easy?"

Vail grunted. "Wait here, then." The marshal left his desk and went out to the waiting room, leaving Longarm alone in the marshal's private office for only a moment. When he came back Vail was carrying a slim sheaf of papers Longarm recognized as case-report forms.

"This came in yesterday," Vail said, resuming his seat behind his desk and pulling out a pair of reading spectacles so he could refresh himself on the case before handing the papers to Longarm. "I was going to send Adams on this one, but he's been out in the field for nearly a month already, and his wife gets upset when he spends too much time away from home."

Longarm said nothing. His private opinion was that a deputy marshal had no business encumbering himself with a nervous wife—or any kind of wife, for that matter. Too distracting, he thought. On the other hand, he admitted to himself, his opinion on the subject might well be different if he himself ever met a woman he truly did not want to live without. He was a bachelor by choice, but he was not foolish enough to believe that he or any other man was completely immune from matrimony. It was just that it had not yet happened to him. The fact that he liked it that way was neither here nor there. He was entirely too bright to make any pronouncements in absolute terms, if only because everything is subject to change at any unexpected moment.

Vail finished re-reading the case report and tossed it across the desk where Longarm could reach it. "This one should be pretty simple and straightforward," the marshal said. "Murder. A government survey crew from the Bureau of Land Management...that's under Interior, by the way...got themselves wiped out. Somewhere east of Monument and north of Peyton."

"Indians?" Longarm asked skeptically. It was the first thought that came to mind, though it had been some years since there had been serious Indian trouble this far south. There were still potential problems in the territories to the north, but even there there was more fear than threat. And what problems there were were mostly minor ones.

Billy Vail shook his head. "Nope. According to the information we got, a small group of men riding shod horses came into their camp and cut loose on them at close range with shotguns. There were four men in the party. I understand they were shot up pretty bad."

"Survivors?"

"Not a chance. It was a very thorough job."

"Motive?"

"Obviously there had to be one. There always is. But damned if I can figure what it might have been. Unless one or more of those boys made a real hard effort at working up some enemies."

"Revenge is a nice motive," Longarm agreed, "but greed is usually a better one. This survey crew wouldn't have been mapping gold discoveries or something like that, would they?"

"I think in this case you'd have to stretch it to find greed for a motive," Vail said. "They were doing a topographic survey."

"What the hell is one of them?"

"Determining ground contours and making maps," Vail explained. "It was a watershed survey, actually. They were trying to pinpoint exactly where the Arkansas Divide is."

"I've heard of the Continental Divide, of course, but the Arkansas Divide is a new one on me."

"Same principle," Vail said, "but in this instance there is a smaller area involved. The Continental Divide is the separation between the Atlantic and Pacific Oceans. For watershed purposes, that is. The Arkansas Divide is the separation between the Arkansas River watershed and the Platte River. South Platte, to be more precise."

"So, who cares?"

"A few little men in the BLM offices, the kind who wear eyeshades and sleeve garters and think the government would cease to function without them. At least, they are the ones who hired the survey crew and sent them out to make their maps. Beyond that, I really don't know who would care. *I* certainly don't. No, this time, Longarm, I think I'd look for someone who had a real mad on for one or more of those boys in the survey crew. It could be our killers set out to murder one of the boys and had to kill the rest to avoid discovery."

"*Try* to avoid discovery," the lean deputy amended. "I'll try and see that they don't succeed at it."

"You want the job, then?"

"Billy, right now I'd snap at the job of escorting a train of manure wagons to Rhode Island. Any damn thing that'll get me out of Denver and away from that fat female with her moonstruck calf eyes."

"I don't have anything quite like that available at the moment, Longarm, but I can check around and..."

Longarm stood quickly and snatched up the sheaf of papers. "I'll read this over before I head out, Billy."

"That would be nice."

Longarm started out the door.

"Custis."

He stopped and turned. "Yes, Billy?"

"Do remember to send an appropriate note of apology to the congressman and his family. The gentleman hasn't any important committee assignments in Washington at the moment, but you never know what next year might bring, if you know what I mean."

Longarm sighed. "Yes, boss." There were times—very nearly all of the time, in fact—when he was mighty glad he did not have to care about politics or the avoidance of political toes that might get stepped on. Not that Billy Vail was overly concerned with that himself. And never to the point of allowing politics to interfere with the job at hand. It was just that Vail was a prudent man when prudence was called for and was convenient. Longarm was glad he did not have to be.

"I'll send the note this morning," Longarm promised. He left the office, feeling much better than he had when he had arrived.

Chapter 2

By the time Longarm read through the case report and jotted down some notes for himself, went back to his rooming house near Cherry Creek for his traveling gear, and found a hack to take him to the railroad station, he was barely in time to catch the southbound 11:15 for Monument.

He climbed awkwardly into the day coach, encumbered by his valise, McClellan saddle, and Winchester, and stowed his gear on the overhead rack. The steam engine was already beginning to lurch forward uncertainly amid loud clankings of steel couplings and much hissing of steam before he got settled in the coal-grimed seat he would occupy for the next several hours.

A boy of eight or ten wearing short britches and no shoes was still on board, trying to hawk a last copy or two of the *Denver Post* early edition before he would have to quit the car and jump off while he still could, before the passenger train picked up too much speed. Longarm gave the kid a nickel, got a smile and a newspaper in return but no change, and watched the boy race for the exit at the last possible second. Longarm was not sure if he should admire the kid's grit or yell at him for not offering change. The offer would have been refused, but it should have been made.

The uniformed Denver & Rio Grande conductor came through the car moments later to collect tickets and pass out information. Longarm showed his rail pass—thanks to right-of-way land grants and mail contracts, certain classes of federal employees were entitled to ride free—and sat back with the newspaper in his lap.

He was not entirely sure Billy Vail would approve of Longarm's decision to take a train south for this job. And Longarm had been most careful not to bring that subject under discussion.

The country north and east from Colorado Springs was marginally close enough that Longarm could have elected or been ordered to draw a horse from the army's remount service depot in Denver and travel in that inexpensive manner.

The advantage from Vail's point of view would have been that use of the Army nags was free; there would have been no expense involved in hiring a horse. The disadvantage from Longarm's was that the damned remount boys nearly always stuck him with the sorriest animal they happened to have on hand at any given moment.

By taking the train south and renting a horse at the first convenient livery he came to, he could be reasonably sure of obtaining a decent animal to use.

Besides, he justified the choice to himself, this way he would be on the crime scene a solid day earlier than would otherwise have been possible. He made a mental note to

11

remind Vail of that fact when he turned in his expense voucher for the marshal's approval.

He lit a cheroot, crossed his legs, and began to scan the newspaper. Almost immediately an expression of distaste pulled his lips tight and narrowed his eyes.

Damn lawyers, he thought with disgust. *Most of them, if not quite all. And, come to think of it, maybe all of them.*

In the lower right-hand corner of the front page there was an item briefly stating that the federal trial of C. A. Watson, accused of murder, had this morning resulted in a mistrial based on defense motions prior to the scheduled closing arguments. The short article did not specify on what grounds the mistrial had been declared, and Longarm did not particularly want to know.

He did do some cursing under his breath, though. Now the whole case would have to be rescheduled and heard all over again. As chief witness for the prosecution—he had been *very* careful with the physical evidence that was necessary for Watson's eventual conviction—Longarm would have to spend more dreary time on the witness stand at some time in the future. He had done it often enough before, of course, but it was a part of the job he did not relish.

Longarm knew good and well how it would go all over again, especially with the kind of defense Watson's highly paid attorney was mounting. The prosecutor would ask a question. Before Longarm could answer, the defense would voice an objection. Both lawyers would expound their points before the judge. Eventually the judge would tire of the charade and make a ruling on the objection. And then, half an hour or so after the question had been asked, Longarm might—or might not—be told to go ahead and answer the damn thing.

For a lawman who genuinely believed in justice, trials

12

could be damned frustrating.

At least in the meantime, though, Watson would be kept behind bars, where he quite thoroughly belonged. The *Post* article did say that a defense motion for release of the prisoner until the new trial had been denied.

Longarm sighed. The Watson case could be hanging over him for months to come. If only, he mused, the rich little bastard hadn't been bright enough to surrender quietly and immediately holler for his lawyer when Longarm took him in custody. It would have saved quite an amount of time and money too if the little shit had stood up and fought like a man instead of surrendering with that syrup-sweet meekness and that damned smirk on his freshly shaved face. Longarm got mad every time he thought of Watson, or anyone else for that matter whose meannesses were confined to defenseless women.

Watson's history contained only one recorded instance when the man's viciousness had been let loose on a grown man. And then Watson had shot the poor fellow in the back of the head from close range. That time his lawyer had, incredibly enough, succeeded in pleading self-defense, making a mockery of the territorial judicial system in Dakota Territory but somehow getting away with it.

That case, Longarm thought, was kind of like the one down in Reconstruction Texas where the old boy committed suicide by wrapping himself in forty feet of trace chain, shooting himself four times in the back, and then jumping into the well of his farm. Kind of made a fellow wonder. But the official ruling that time had been suicide, and once it was on the books that was all there was to it.

Well, Longarm mused, Watson was going to get himself a surprise if he thought the United States attorney for the Denver district wasn't going to bother with a retrial. And no matter how long the damn trial was put off, in the end Mr. Watson was going to hang. Deputy U. S. Marshal Custis Long intended to see to it just as personally as he possibly could.

Angry now and feeling rather bitter, Longarm tossed the newspaper aside and sat in sullen silence for the remainder of the trip down to Monument.

He knew they were approaching the small town well before the conductor passed through the cars to announce the stop. There was a labored uphill climb as the Denver & Rio Grande engine breasted Monument Hill, then a downward rush with the brakes set and squealing in protest to bring the cars to a halt on the flat land where the town had been built.

Longarm had not particularly thought about it before but now, in the light of his current assignment, he realized that Monument Hill, immediately north of Monument and Palmer Lake, was probably the western end of the Arkansas Divide those murdered survey crewmen had been mapping for the government. He would have to check, but that certainly stood to reason.

The train clattered finally to a halt, and Longarm gathered his gear and swung down to the cinder-and-gravel roadbed, avoiding the depot platform with its baggage trucks and confusion. Monument was no great shakes as a town, but it was the stopping point for passengers on their way to the baths and picnic grounds at Palmer Lake, where so many of Denver's swells liked to take the air. The railway station here was frequently busy far out of proportion to the size of the community.

Longarm walked to the livery a block distant from the train depot and took a minute or two to look over the selection available before he approached the old fellow who was tending the place.

"I seen you look 'em over," the hostler said, "so likely you got your mind set on one." He turned his head aside and spat, just missing a pair of sleepy flies with his stream of yellow tobacco juice.

"Nope." Longarm grinned at the old man. "I expect you know them better'n I could. So I reckon I could listen to a recommendation, if you want to make one."

"Well, I'll be damned." The old fellow stood and walked with Longarm back to the corral where a dozen head of horses were lazing in the sunshine. "Most folks figger they already know it all," he said.

"I thought I did too, but I was wrong once. Don't want that to happen a second time." Longarm leaned on the top rail. He fished a pair of cheroots from his pocket and offered one to the hostler, who declined it. Longarm put it away and lit one for himself.

"D'ya see that black over there?"

"Uh-huh. It's the horse I'd have picked. If I was doing the picking without advice, that is."

The old man grunted with obvious satisfaction. "Most ever' damn body wants him. The idjits like him 'cause he's pretty. Fellas that know horses, they like the way he's built. Good-lookin' son of a bitch, ain't he?"

"So what's wrong with him?"

"Stumbled footed. Dumb bastard can't walk ten rod without tryin' to fall down. I'd shoot him, except I make so much money off him that I can't afford to."

"I appreciate you telling me."

The old man shrugged. "Most don't ask. An' them as does, most don't listen. Figger I'm tryin' to save him for special or somethin'. Hell, boy, I don't care what horse a fella takes outa here. The price's the same, so it don't matter none to me."

"So what's your recommendation?"

15

"You see that little bay off in the corner there?"

"Yep."

"That right there is the best I got. She's a mare, though. If you're too proud to ride a mare, why, I'll find you another. But that little mare, she's steady. Not the least bit notional, and she'll go all day. I'd say she goes nine hundred pound, and eight hundred of that's got to be heart. A man could ride her down an' kill her, but he couldn't use her so bad that she'd quit on him."

"She sounds like she'll do," Longarm said.

The old man ducked and slipped into the corral between the rails. Most of the horses ignored him. The black Longarm had been admiring pinned its ears and tried to hide behind the rest of the small herd. The short-coupled bay mare, Longarm noticed, took a few steps toward the handler. When he headed her way she tossed her head and whickered, then stood quietly waiting for him to claim her. Longarm opened the gate and the hostler led her outside.

"She stands tied just fine," the old fellow said as he handed her over to Longarm. "You can tie her to a twig an' she'll be there most of forever if need be. There's some say she ground-ties too, but I don't claim it." He grinned. "Walked too damn many miles chasin' horses I thought would ground-tie to trust another. Course, you do what you want."

"Thank you."

"Usin' her long?"

Longarm shrugged. "No idea. I'll bring her back or send her back when I'm done." He reached in a coat pocket for a claim chit. "Write the charges down here when you know what they are and send it in. The address is printed right here on the form. The government will send you a check."

"Don't like checks," the old man grumped.

"Uncle is good for it. Uh . . . most tack on a couple dollars for their trouble in waiting for the pay."

The old man scowled, obviously not at all mollified by that suggestion.

"If that isn't enough," Longarm suggested, "I'll give you my personal promise to come back and make it good if the government doesn't."

The old fellow brightened and nodded. "That sounds better."

Longarm tacked the mare with his own saddle and bridle, strapped the Winchester in its scabbard to the straps on the McClellan, and stepped into the saddle. The mare offered no resistance to the handling and made no effort to move off when Longarm mounted. That in itself was going to be a pleasure.

"Boy," said the old man.

"Yes, sir?"

"This paper you gave me."

"Yes, sir?"

"I ain't gonna add nothing to it that I ain't rightfully earned. I want you should know that."

Longarm smiled at him. "Yes, sir. I expect I do know that." He reined the little mare toward the center of the small town and touched his spurs lightly to her sides. She moved off with calm obedience.

Chapter 3

The matronly woman who was waiting tables in the small eatery paused in the middle of pouring Longarm's coffee and thought for a moment. "Hansen? Oh, what's the matter with me? Of course I remember the child. Birgita. But her name isn't Hansen any longer. That's what threw me, you see. She married the oldest Lichter boy. They live..." She paused and gave Longarm a suspicious second look. "Did you say you know the child?"

Longarm's memory of Birgita Hansen, from the last time his work had brought him to Monument, was hardly that of a child. But then the matronly woman's point of view would be different from what his had been. He could remember quite well how delightful the pretty little blonde Norska had been. She had not been at all childlike.

"I met her before in the line of duty, ma'am," Longarm said. It was not exactly a lie. He introduced himself, and the woman's expression softened.

"I see," she said. "Like I told you, the child married Tommy Lichter. They're living south of here, in Pikeview. I could give you directions if you like."

Longarm smiled and shook his head. "No need, ma'am, although I thank you for the offer. She just seemed like a very lovely...uh...child, and I was wondering how she was. I'm glad she found a young man."

"They seem real happy," the woman said, filling his cup and gathering the dirty dishes that remained from his slightly late lunch.

"Glad to hear that," Longarm said.

It was true enough. She had been a real joy to be with, but he had staked no claims. If she had found happiness in a permanent attachment, he was genuinely pleased for her.

As for coming back here for his dinner, well, a man did have to eat. He could not say he would have minded if he had found Birgita still here and still willing, but the fact that she was not was equally acceptable.

"Her and her man still come up here once in a while. Should I tell her you was asking after her, Deputy?"

"Please do." Longarm hoped she would not misunderstand that, would not feel threatened or embarrassed that he had asked after her welfare, but he was sure any other answer would have led to much more misunderstanding than that. If he asked this woman *not* to give his respects to the now-married girl, he would be as good asking for rumors to start. And that he certainly would not wish on anyone he liked.

Apparently satisfied, the woman accepted Longarm's money for his meal and left him alone with his coffee and cigar.

As soon as he was finished, Longarm wandered out of the little restaurant. He left the mare tied where she was at

19

the hitch rail in front of the place and walked down the block to the combination saloon and general store. The two were under one roof but divided by a wall into separate businesses.

He entered the saloon, nearly empty at this time of day, and asked about the survey crewmen.

"Nope," the barman said, "I don't recall meeting anyone by those names in here. If they'd been working aroun' here any time recent, I'm sure I'd have got to know them."

Longarm thanked the man and left without taking time for a drink.

The bodies had been brought in to Peyton, so apparently the men had been working well to the east of here when they were murdered. The barman, Norm, did not even seem to have heard about the shootings. Or if he had it had not been of local enough interest for the names to take hold in his memory.

The logical thing to do, Longarm thought, would be to follow the Arkansas Divide east from Monument Hill and see what he could come up with.

But no one knew really where the damn thing ran, which was the reason for the survey. Trying to backtrack the survey crew, then, he would have to begin with the site where they were killed.

He went back to the bay mare and swung onto her, well aware that it was already too late in the day for him to reach Peyton by horseback.

He thought briefly about taking a Denver & Rio Grande train south, switching at Colorado City to an eastbound Kansas Pacific, and riding it on to Peyton. But the trouble and expense seemed hardly worth the bother, since he had no idea what kind of connections he could expect. Besides, by going overland he could tell Billy Vail how much money he had saved the office by not shipping the mare—he could ride free, but the non-government horse would not—and demonstrate all over again what a thoughtful fellow he was.

In truth, he could have gone faster and cheaper yet by turning the horse back to the livery and riding the trains on his rail pass. But, damn it, he wanted to keep the little mare, since he was certain to need the use of a horse for most of this investigation. After some of the remount nags that had been wished off on him, the little bay was a real treat.

With his valise strapped on behind the cantle and provisions enough to last a day or so, he rode east and south from the small town at the edge of the Front Range.

Shortly before dusk Longarm began looking for a good place to camp, following the lip of one of the countless dry washes that crisscrossed the country here until he found what he wanted.

He was not looking for a place to stop down in the wash. Entirely too many fools had been drowned by ignoring the perfectly obvious fact that a deep, steep-walled wash was caused by water, lots of water running fast and hard. Too many had camped on the soft, dry sands of such a wash and woke up dead when a wall of swift water came racing down on them in their sleep.

But the same raging—and rare—water that digs washes and sometimes drowns people also carries with it large amounts of debris, including driftwood. With trees and dry wood as scarce as opera houses out on the open grass, the washes are a good place to search for firewood.

Longarm found what he was looking for, a snag of brittle driftwood lodged against a nest of low boulders, and climbed down to retrieve the wood for his evening fire.

He used one short chunk driven into the hard soil as a

stake to tie the mare and piled the rest on the ground. There were no terrain features in sight that could serve as a windbreak—except, of course, for the walls of the wash—so one place seemed quite as good as another.

There was not enough cactus here to worry about either. The Great Southwestern Desert, so-called, with its scanty rainfall and spiny growth, began not more than a dozen miles south of where Longarm stopped, but here the soil was loosely covered with bunch grasses and occasional clumps of yucca or soapweed. A very few button cactus could be found. There was not an actual tree anywhere within sight.

Longarm shared his water with the mare and whittled slivers from the softest bits of driftwood to use for kindling. Within moments he had a small, cheery fire alight.

He really did not need a fire. Supper would be jerky and cold biscuits, and he did not feel like bothering to brew a can of coffee for himself after his late dinner. But the fire took some of the chill out of the evening air and pushed back the falling night. It was too early to go to sleep, but too dark to travel country he did not know. He rummaged in his valise for the bottle of Maryland rye he customarily carried and leaned back against the seat of the McClellan.

He ate a little of the cold food and followed it with the clean taste and belly-warming pleasure of the good rye.

Already the quick-burning driftwood was flickering low, so he leaned forward to feed the fire.

Out of the corner of his eye he saw the mare's head jerk upward from her grazing, and the soft, grinding sound of her chewing ceased.

Without thinking it out, Longarm rolled to the side.

A rifle slug sizzled past with the buzzing snarl that a three-pound bumblebee would probably make. The slug gouged a furrow in the hard caliche soil on the far side of the fire and went whining off into the night. It was at least a full second later before Longarm heard the report from the distant rifle. He was positive it was a rifle, because the shot was too long to be attempted with a handgun.

By the time the sound of the shot reached him, Longarm was yards away, crawling on his belly and wishing he had thought to grab the Winchester from its boot before he scuttled out of the firelight.

He was also cursing himself for his own damn-foolishness because after looking into the fire while he fed it seconds before he had completely ruined his night vision. It would be long seconds more before he could see worth a damn.

The double-action Colt .44 Thunderer was in his hand, but he had no hope at all that he would be able to do anything with it.

Not unless the unknown rifleman thought Longarm was hit and came in to see.

That was a slim hope at best, because the man out there in the darkness would certainly be able to see that his intended victim had crawled away from the fire.

On the other hand, it was just about the only hope Longarm had of being able to come to grips with the man.

If Longarm went back into the firelight for the Winchester, he would be an ideal target for a second shot. It wouldn't pay to trust to the other fellow's bad luck or poor aim. Longarm had probably already used up his entire day's quota of good luck when the mare saw something—likely the muzzle flash when the rifle fired—and reacted to it.

The temptation was to try to stalk the rifleman, particularly once his night vision returned, but it was generally unwise to face a rifleman with nothing but a revolver. The limits of accuracy were simply weighted too heavily in the other man's favor.

So Longarm lay motionless and silent on the hard ground and waited. Half an hour after the last red gleam had died from his campfire, he concluded that the rifleman, whoever he had been, was long gone.

All of that time Longarm had been pondering the same question. Who the hell could it have been?

The same party who gunned down the survey crew? That seemed unlikely. He had not yet even reached Peyton to begin his investigation.

Yet he *had* asked the barman back in Monument about the dead surveyors, so it was at least possible that someone knew he was here to investigate the murders.

Had he told the bartender he was a deputy marshal? He could not remember. And even if he had not, that was no guarantee, since it was at least remotely possible that the man remembered him from the last time Longarm had been in Monument on official business.

And if it was *not* because of some freak of coincidence that let the guilty parties find out about his investigation so soon after he arrived, then he could not think who in the hell the rifleman could possibly have been.

After all, there were a fair number of people in this world who did not care for people of Longarm's profession. But damn few of them went around shooting every law officer they saw.

No, he finally decided, as improbable and unfortunate as it was, it was most likely that someone had learned of his interest in the dead surveyors and was trying to head off the investigation by knocking off the investigator.

And the worst part of it all, Longarm thought, was that this bastard, whoever he was, was almighty good. Because whoever he was and for whatever reason he had just tried to kill a deputy United States marshal, the bastard had followed Longarm all afternoon long, *and never once had Longarm realized that anyone was trailing him.*

The knowledge that he was being hunted by someone that good was absolutely the most worrisome fact of all.

Longarm waited until he was absolutely, positively, guaranteed certain sure that the rifleman was no longer in the area, then waited half an hour more and saddled the bay. Whatever else might happen, he was not going to sit in the same spot until daylight and give the bastard another chance.

Chapter 4

Longarm developed even more respect—if it could be called that—for the unknown rifleman come daylight. He spent the remainder of the night without a fire several miles distant from the place where he had been discovered and shot at, but at first light he made his way carefully back to the site.

He had not seen exactly where the shot was fired from, but he knew the approximate direction to follow away from the ashes that had been his campfire. It took more than half an hour to find the place where the rifleman must have been.

There was little enough evidence to tell him that he had found the correct location. A faint disturbance of the dry grass stems might have been caused by the rifleman lying down to take aim from a solid, prone position or by an antelope bedding for the night. A few scuff marks could have been caused by boot toes digging into the ground just there or by a pawing hoof. Some yards away there was a pile of fresh horse manure. The manure was not strung out, as it would have been if the animal had been moving... but it could have been left by some cowhand's mount when the man stopped to roll a smoke.

There was no way to tell for sure. But Longarm believed that this faint rise in the rolling terrain, no more than half a dozen feet higher than the place where his camp had been, was the most logical place from which the shot could have been fired.

The distance told him nothing about the weapon the rifleman had used. It was two hundred yards out, perhaps a shade closer. Long but reasonable distance for a saddle carbine, well within normal range for a Sharps or Remington or even a Winchester with a rifle-length barrel.

What told him the most about this unknown adversary, though, was what he did *not* find at the scene.

There was no empty cartridge case to be found on the flint-hard soil.

Either the rifleman had not reloaded after firing—something that Longarm did not believe for a moment—or the man had been cautious enough, and smart enough, to pick up his empty brass once it was ejected.

And caution of that nature smacked of a professionalism Longarm did not like.

It was not that he was a coward. Far from that. But no sensible man relishes the thought of being the target of ambush. All the less so if the ambusher is wise to the ways of the ugly profession of the assassin.

Longarm believed himself the equal of any man in nearly any kind of fight. If he ever lost that confidence he would know it would be time to leave the business of law enforcement and seek a tamer field. But with an ambusher there might never be a fight, because the ambusher had all the advantages of stealth and concealment and patience. And his target could do little to defend himself if there was already a bullet in his back before he knew there was danger about.

This rifleman had already demonstrated his willingness to backshoot from hiding.

Until this business was done, Longarm knew, he would never be able to allow himself a moment's relaxation, because the final bullet could fly unexpected from any clump of brush, any rotting tree stump, any distant knoll.

The tall deputy stood on the low mound and scanned the horizon with the wistful but unrealized wish that this rifleman, whoever he might be, would come out into the open and get it done with. But there was nothing there to see, nothing but a bright and cloudless sky, the browning grassland of the late summer, and the distant mountains lying tall and cool and rugged to the west.

With a grunt, Longarm swung back onto the mare and turned her once again toward Peyton.

He entered the little tank town from the west. Since he did not know precisely where Peyton lay in relation to Monument he had found it the easy way, riding southeast until he felt he should go no farther, then traveling due south until he reached the wheel-polished steel of the railroad tracks. All he had to do then was turn east and follow the rails to Peyton. Directly behind him, although it was a good many miles away, the bald knob of Pikes Peak loomed over his shoulder.

Peyton was both small and sprawling, its tiny business section clustered around the railroad depot which was more shed than station, open on the side facing the tracks and with a small platform of planks built between the shed and the trackside, its few houses sprouting in an apparently haphazard pattern over a half-mile radius around the depot. A complex of corrals and loading chutes had been built at the southeast corner of the town immediately adjacent to the tracks, giving a clear indication of what the area's primary occupation would be: cattle would be loaded there and hauled to the markets in the East.

That was probably the major industry of the community and its surrounding area, but a quick look showed that it was not the sole endeavor here. Probably because the railroad gave easy access to the local markets at Colorado Springs, Colorado City, Manitou, and Fountain, there were also extensive plots of vegetables planted amid the scattered houses. As he rode in he could also see two small herds of Jersey-bred dairy cattle, virtually useless for beef but producers of high-quality milk and butter.

It seemed like a peaceful, pleasant town, dominated by the railroad's huge windmill and water tank, sleepy and seemingly content in the midday sunshine. It was hardly the sort of place one would associate with murder.

Longarm passed by the tiny depot and rode into the business district. There was a large general mercantile and next to it the livery with a public corral between them. Past the livery was a small grainery. All of those were on the side of the street nearest the railroad tracks.

Across the street were several smaller businesses including a barbershop, smithy, restaurant, and, at the far end of the section—it would have been too formal to call it a block—a single saloon.

On the north side of the town, separate from the businesses but not quite included among the homes, was a white-painted church with a curiously shaped cross standing proud above a squat steeple. Longarm had seen that form of cross before. He could not remember what it was supposed to be called, but he did remember that it indicated a Russian or Greek influence.

He paused first beneath the water tank to let the bay mare drink from the public trough that had been provided there, then led her across the street and tied her in front of the clapboard shack that had a sign hung out front proclaiming "Eats," "Sanwitch & Coffee 10¢," "Full Meal 25¢." It had been a long time since breakfast, and meals of jerky and old biscuits were more filling than they were satisfying.

The restaurant was run by a middle-aged man with one arm. Longarm did not have to guess how the man had lost his right arm. A faded daguerreotype was hung on the wall over the cash box and below it a blue cap with artillery brass and red piping. The place was cleaner and looked to be better run than many Longarm had seen in similar small towns.

"G'day," the proprietor greeted.

"Howdy." Longarm removed his Stetson and hung it on a peg beside the front door. "Looks like I missed the lunch crowd. I hope you're still serving."

"Yep."

"What's your full meal today?"

"Beef stew. The vegetables are fresh. Local grown they are. An' it won't turn your stomach, even if I do say so myself."

Longarm smiled and took a seat at the short counter rather than choosing one of the few tables. "It sounds good and you look like you know what you're doing here, but I had my mind kinda set on a steak with some fried taters."

"Thirty-five cents for that," the man said.

"Fair enough."

The man disappeared into a back room and returned a

moment later with a thick slab of raw meat and two potatoes. He slapped the meat onto the already hot stove and began to chop the potatoes. Longarm watched with interest. The fellow worked with a surprising efficiency, using a cleaver to slice the spuds into pieces of uniform thickness. He tossed the slices into a skillet of grease and turned to lean against his counter while he waited for the food to cook.

"Coffee while you wait?" he asked.

"I could use some."

"So could I, if you don't mind the company."

"My pleasure," Longarm said. He extended his left hand to shake and introduced himself.

"Jacob Faust," the one-armed man said, shaking Longarm's hand with a powerful grip. He poured the coffee for both of them and dug into a pocket beneath his surprisingly clean apron for a pouch of flake tobacco and a fold of cigarette papers. He seemed to consider it no trick at all to build a smoke one-handed, lick it closed, and jam it into the corner of his mouth. Longarm watched the performance closely.

Faust shook his match out, opened the firebox door on his stove, and tossed the spent stick inside. "You say you're a U. S. marshal?"

"Just a deputy, but yes, I am."

"Here about them murders, I suppose."

"Uh-huh."

"Well, I hope you find whoever done it. Those were some pretty decent boys."

"You knew them, I take it."

"Yep. They came down here, oh, four, five times I'd say. Taking a little break from the open, picking up supplies, like that. They always came in here to eat when they were in town. Like I said, nice boys. Friendly."

31

"That's one of the things I want to ask about, Mr. Faust."

"Jacob," the man corrected.

"All right. And I'm Custis. Longarm to my friends."

Faust gave him a wry grin. "Longarm an' One-arm. We could team up an' go on stage if one of us could sing. Course, it'd have to be you doin' the singing. I can't tote a tune in a poke myself."

"I think we're sunk then, Jacob." He thought for a moment and, since Faust did not seem particularly sensitive about the old injury, added, "Unless you want to put together a juggling act."

Faust put his head back and roared. "For a government man, Longarm, maybe you aren't totally useless."

Longarm grinned and pointed. "And for a cook, Jacob, maybe you're a pretty fair charcoal maker."

"Oops." Faust grabbed up a long-handled fork and flipped the steak over. The meat had been starting to smoke around the edges. He used the same implement to stir the skillet of potatoes.

"Would you mind if I ask about those boys on the survey crew?" Longarm asked.

Faust grunted. "Hell, man, anything I can do to help, you just ask it. I liked them boys."

"What I'm doing," Longarm explained, "is looking for a motive for somebody to kill them. Mind you, Jacob, I'm not coming in here trying to find fault with them. But what I need to know is whether all of them or, for that matter, any single one of them might have gotten crossways with somebody hereabouts. If one of them might have been a troublemaker or was accused of cheating at cards... anything that might make somebody want to plug him."

"The answer right off the top of my head is that it wouldn't have been that way, Longarm. I already told you, they were a bunch of real friendly boys. Now, I didn't get to know them well, you understand. Just to talk to in here a bit. But a man hears things when people talk amongst themselves. And the way I figured it from the things I heard an' a few things where I kind of filled in the blank places myself, they were college boys from back East somewhere an' one of them had a daddy who got them this job till it was time to go back home an' go back to school. I mean, they just weren't the rowdy kind. For sure they never got loud in here an' never used rough language in front of ladies or nothing like that."

"Did they drink much?"

"I can say they never showed up drunk at suppertime. What they done after that I couldn't say. But if they did carry a heavy load—an' most any kid will when you turn him loose away from home—they never got to the point where there was talk of it in town afterward. Small place, you kind of hear a lot. I never heard talk about them getting out of line. If it was anything real serious, I'd expect to hear about it no later than breakfast the next morning."

"Not serious to the town, then, but that doesn't rule out something that would be serious to some individual."

"That's true enough," Faust agreed. He turned and forked the slab of well-done steak onto a platter, then used a slotted spoon to scoop the fried potatoes out of their bubbling grease and add them on top of the meat. "Is this about what you had in mind?"

"Perfect."

"That meat's what you might call crisp on the one side. If it's too done for you I can fry you another."

Longarm tried a bite. "Nope. This is just fine, Jacob."

"If you're sure."

"Couldn't be happier with it." He dug into the meal with pleasure.

"A minute ago," Longarm went on as he applied a knife

33

to the steak, "you said something about your answer to that question being off the top of your head. Was that a figure of speech, or did you have something else in mind then?"

"Oh . . . nothing, really."

"A man never knows when the little nothing things will turn out to be more interesting than you'd first think." He speared a chunk of the meat with his fork and chewed on the good, grease-fried beef.

"I doubt it would in this case."

Longarm shrugged and went on eating while he waited for Faust to continue. After a moment the man did so.

"One of the last times the boys were in here—might have been the last time, but I couldn't say for sure—I heard one of them say that he thought he was gonna just perish if the Logan girl wouldn't go to the dance with him the next Saturday. Like I said, I'm sure it don't mean anything at all."

"You're probably right, but I'll want to ask around, of course. You don't know if this girl went to the dance or if there might've been some jealousy involved there, do you?"

Faust shook his head. "My missus an me don't go to the dances much. She's down with the arthritis nowadays an' it grieves her to watch them dancing an' her not be able to get in there an' join them. So we mostly stay at home."

"You said the girl's name is Logan?"

"Yep. First name's Emmaline. Linny for short. If she has a regular beau, or anybody that thinks he ought to be, I don't know about it. In fact, she don't seem to have much to do with any of the boys hereabouts, although she's pretty enough that you'd think she'd have them buzzing around her like flies on honey. Most of the local fellows have about decided she's a pretty cold fish an' leave her be. What I think it is, they've all asked to the point they've got tired of being turned down."

34

Longarm grunted. Faust's scrap of information did not sound like a promising lead, but he would have to check it out just to be sure. Nearly all of the work of any investigation was useless and boring. But it could not be considered a waste of time and *never* could be neglected, because a man just never knew exactly which pan of sodden mud would turn out to have flecks of bright gold hidden deep in the brown slop.

Longarm finished his meal with satisfaction, chatted with Jacob Faust a few minutes longer, paid, and left.

He decided to wait and approach the saloon later, when there would be more activity there. In the meantime he would see if he could find the local law or, barring that, look up Linny Logan.

Chapter 5

"Nope. Don't have a town marshal," the blacksmith told Longarm, using his tongs to reposition a cherry-red bit of iron on his anvil and whack it one with his hammer. Longarm had no idea what the metal would eventually become. "No need for one. We do got us a county deputy, though. No office. He lives here. Yonder." The smith nodded vaguely toward the north while he shifted the iron back into the forge for reheating.

"Where might I find the deputy?" Longarm asked.

"Can't." The blacksmith pulled twice on the handle of the huge overhead bellows, sending a gout of fresh air into the belly of the forge. The bed of burning coals puffed sparks and glowed a brighter red, quickly bringing the metal back to a workable temperature. The smith laid a steel mandrel on the anvil, retrieved the iron from the forge, and placed it atop the mandrel. A few more quick strokes of the hammer, and a strap hinge began to emerge.

"What?"

The smith used his tongs to flip the partially made hinge over and whacked it again, and there was a pin channel formed where the mandrel lay trapped inside the still-hot iron. "The deppity ain't here," he told Longarm. "Seen him ride out this morning. He'll be back by dark if he's comin' back. Sometime in the next couple days for sure."

"I see."

"Anything else you want?" He tossed the newly made hinge onto a bench and began pawing through a wooden crate holding oddments of unformed iron, apparently looking for something of a size or shape to suit his fancy for the next bit of work.

"Those boys on the survey crew," Longarm said.

"What survey crew?"

"The ones that were murdered."

"Oh. Them." It was hardly the same kind of interested, helpful response Longarm had gotten from Jacob Faust. "What about 'em?"

"Did you know them?"

"Seen them. Couldn't say that I *knowed* them. Didn't do no business here." It sounded like an accusation more than an explanation.

"Do you know anything about them?"

"Yep."

Longarm waited for the man to go on, but all he went on with was his search in the box of iron pieces. Finally the tall deputy marshal decided he was going to have to play the smith's game and ask the perfectly obvious. "What is it you know about them?"

"They was murdered." The small man—he was not the stereotypical picture of a village smithy—managed to look somewhat smug. He did not look in Longarm's direction to answer, keeping his attention on the crate of scraps.

"Thank you very much," Longarm said, careful to keep any inflection of sarcasm from reaching his voice.

"Any time." The smith still did not look at him.

Longarm went elsewhere to ask directions to the Logan residence.

The Logan house was a small, tidy affair surrounded by a freshly painted white picket fence, inside the boundaries of which the ground was thickly planted with flowers and shrubs. A few spindly saplings, their bases damp with what would have to be a daily effort to keep them watered, gave a promise of shade in the distant sometime. Longarm let himself in through the gate and walked up a graveled, flower-bordered path to the front stoop. The door swung open before he had time to knock.

"Yes?"

Longarm swept his hat off before he answered. The gesture was entirely automatic. It was the only fitting response to the vision that stood before him.

The woman—girl?—was almost too elegant to be believed in this little tank town.

She was tall, very nearly as tall as Longarm, and proportioned like a Greek statue. Her blonde hair was fastened on top of her head in a remarkably intricate coif of curls and swirls. She wore a dress which would have been perfectly appropriate for luncheon in downtown Denver, and her at-home costuming included sparkly earrings and a large cameo suspended on a gold chain necklace. Her nose was patrician, her cheeks a glowing blush of health that might or might not have been enhanced beyond what nature had ordained. Her most arresting feature was her eyes, a bright, bright blue that reminded Longarm of glacier ice under a summer sky.

Her expression was prim and haughty at the same time. Not welcoming—as cold and disinterested as her eyes.

If Longarm had been a young and inexperienced man, far from the accustomed luxuries and refined parlors of the East, he undoubtedly would have been bowled plumb off his feet by this ice maiden. No wonder the boy on the survey crew had been so anxious to take this one for a stepping-out.

As it was, though, Longarm had more important things to think about. "Miss Logan, I presume." It was not really a question.

"I am."

Longarm introduced himself.

"Yes, Marshal?"

"I wondered if I could have a few minutes of your time, miss."

"As you wish, Marshal." She stepped back from the doorframe and motioned him inside.

The Logan parlor was small, scaled to the proportions of the house, and crammed beyond capacity with plush furnishings, carved tables, oil lamps with hand-painted shades and bric-a-brac crowding every available surface. Longarm wondered how much the Logans had to spend on feather dusters every year.

Miss Logan showed him to a seat at one end of an over-stuffed sofa with gilt lion's-paw feet and herself chose to sit at the other end of the same sofa, although a number of comfortable-looking chairs were nearby. She sat with one arm draped with regal affectation on the back of the sofa. She looked at Longarm with her head tilted slightly back and waited patiently for him to initiate the conversation. She did not offer him a beverage or snack, as was the custom here.

"I'm here investigating the murder of those boys on the

government survey crew, Miss Logan."

"Yes?" Again she waited. There were no exclamations of "how awful," no clucking sympathy. She volunteered nothing at all.

"I have reason to believe, Miss Logan," Longarm said easily, "that you were acquainted with at least one of the murdered boys." If this young lady—Longarm guessed her age at about twenty, give a couple years or take one back—thought she was going to weave her spell on him, she was mistaken. Custis Long had been down the path too many times to lose his way casually now.

"And so I was, Marshal." Again she made no effort to elaborate or explain, but simply answered the surface of his implied question and waited for him to go on. She looked cool and quite poised.

"With all of the boys?" he asked.

"I was acquainted, briefly, with the young gentleman from Princeton."

Longarm was able to resist making a comment about snobbery, but his amused expression probably made comment unnecessary. "My report didn't list their schools, Miss Logan. Would it be too much trouble for you to tell me his name?"

"Thomas Henry Harrison," she said. "His family was...is...quite closely connected with that of the ninth president of the United States."

"I see." He did, too—about the girl, if not much about Harrison. He wondered if she realized how revealing her answer was. Probably not.

"Is there anything else you wish to ask, Marshal?" She moved as if she were about to rise and terminate the interview.

Longarm remained where he was, relaxed and perfectly

comfortable. Just for the hell of it, he faked a yawn. "As a matter of fact," he said, "there are a number of other things I need to know."

The girl looked slightly annoyed. "I know nothing about the murders, Marshal. Or are you suggesting that I am a suspect in your investigation?" The question came out heavily freighted with sarcasm.

"I don't know yet," Longarm said seriously. "That will depend on your answers."

Emmaline Logan settled back onto the sofa. She did not look quite so superior now.

"Tell me, Linny—"

"Please," she interrupted. "I detest that nickname."

"Could your...uh...acquaintance," Longarm resumed as if there had been no interruption, "have been resented by any of the local boys?"

She gave him a drop-dead look.

"Could any of them have become jealous of young Harrison's attentions?" Longarm went on.

Again she only gave him a disdainful look.

Longarm smiled at her. Quite calmly he said, "There hasn't been time for a formal inquest to be held, you know. If you'd prefer—and the choice is entirely yours—I can have you subpoenaed and ask my questions when you're under oath."

"You wouldn't."

He shrugged. "Your choice."

She began to look a bit worried. "I have given *no* encouragement to any of the local rubes, Marshal. I can assure you of that."

"Yes, I think you probably can at that." She seemed not to get the point of the small barb contained in his statement. "But you didn't answer my question yet, Linny." He used the nickname deliberately. "Could any of the local boys have been jealous?"

"There should have been no point to it. I believe any of them would have known that."

"But are any of the local boys particularly persistent?"

"Several," she said smugly.

"Names?"

"You cannot be serious."

"You do insist on makin' that mistake, don't you, Linny?"

She wilted slightly. "Alfred Wicks. Possibly Horace Glesson. They are both, as you put it, persistent." She made a face and manufactured a small shudder.

"And you say you know nothing about the murders? You suspect nothing?"

"I do not."

"I may want to question you again, Linny, but that should do for the moment."

Her composure, only briefly weakened, returned now. She gave Longarm another cold look from the vantage point of her—at least in her own opinion—unquestioned superiority. "You are only looking for an excuse to bother me again, Marshal. I know your kind."

Longarm laughed. He supposed it was rude, and he really did not want to burst the poor, dumb, beautiful bitch's bubble, but he couldn't help it. He threw his head back and roared.

She looked offended and surprised.

"Linny," he said, "you'd better do your hunting with the boys, 'cause one of these days you're going to run across a grown-up male, and he's likely to take you across his lap and give you a paddling." Still laughing, Longarm got up and let himself out of the tiny but oddly pretentious Logan house.

Chapter 6

Longarm met the El Paso County sheriff's deputy who was in charge of the entire eastern portion of the sprawlingly large county when he went back to Jacob Faust's eatery for supper. In addition to being ready for a light meal by then, Longarm was more or less forced to return to the restaurant, because Faust had allowed him to leave his valise and Winchester there while the federal deputy wandered around town asking his questions.

"'Lo, Longarm," Faust greeted him.

"Hello, Jacob."

"Do any good this afternoon?"

Longarm shook his head and took a seat at the counter where he had stopped earlier.

"You might wanta move over to that table in the corner," Fasut suggested.

"Really?" The table was already occupied by a young

man wearing a dark gray suit, high-heeled boots worn outside his trousers, and a clean but much-weathered Stetson.

"Unless you've already met Race, that is."

"No, I haven't."

"C'mon." The one-armed cook and proprietor led Longarm to the back table. "Race, this is Deputy Marshal Custis Long, down from Denver to ask about the boys that were killed here. Longarm, this wet-nosed young'un who looks like he couldn't find his own saddle with his butt is Race Glesson, deputy sheriff for these parts." He winked and added, "Kind of shows you what an elected official will wish off on an area that doesn't have many voters."

The young deputy grinned at Faust before he slowly stood and extended a hand for Longarm to shake.

With an introduction like that, Longarm thought, young Race Glesson must be very well liked by the people he served in Peyton and probably was also a highly competent officer of the law.

"My pleasure, Custis," the youngster said.

"Longarm to my friends, Deputy."

"Race to mine. Join me for supper?"

"I'd like that." Longarm pulled out a chair and sat.

He turned to Faust but the man smiled and said, "I know. You'll pass on the stew. Steak and potatoes, right?"

"You got it."

"Damn good thing you said that, Longarm, 'cause I got them cut and waiting to go onto the fire already."

Longarm chuckled. "You're an accommodating host, Mr. Faust. I predict you will go far."

"Yep. All the way to the poor farm if I don't get busy around here." Faust hurried back to his stoves. Even at this busy hour he was handling all of the work himself.

"That seems like a pretty good man going there," Longarm said, turning back to the young deputy.

"You'll find that most of the folks around here are that way," the deputy said. "Good people. They work hard and aren't afraid to help a neighbor." He smiled. "Makes my job pretty easy."

"Uh-huh." Longarm knew how "easy" things could get on a Saturday night when the boys from the surrounding ranches were liquored up and looking for ways to get rid of their pay. But he respected the young man for keeping his complaints and war stories to himself.

"I expect I can guess what brought you down here," Race said.

Longarm nodded. "They were under contract to the Department of the Interior, which gives us an interest in the killings. Naturally we aren't interested in stepping on any toes. If you have it all wrapped up already, I'll be glad to turn around and go home."

"Huh! Wish I could tell you that I did have. The truth is, I'll be glad for any help I can get on this one. I went out to the murder scene, of course. But then you likely already saw the report I sent in on it."

"I did, but I'd like to take a look for myself."

"I'll take you out there in the morning," Race agreed quickly. Longarm was beginning to think he was going to get along with this young fellow nicely. That would be a distinct improvement over a good many of the local yahoos he had had to work with in the past.

Longarm motioned to the half-eaten bowl of stew in front of Race and at the mound of oven-fresh biscuits that had been served with it. "Don't let your supper get cold there. Go ahead."

"All right." Race resumed his meal.

"Did you know any of the boys on that crew?" Longarm asked.

Race nodded and swallowed. "All of them. I couldn't

45

say I knew them well, but I'd spoken to each of them at one time or another."

"Over anything special?"

The youngster had just taken another bite. He shook his head and swallowed before he answered. "I know what you're asking, but they weren't a rowdy bunch. I make it a point to talk to everybody new who comes into the area. You know. Let them know we have some law here in case they have need . . . or cause a need. You likely know how that is."

Longarm nodded. It was a good habit for a local peace officer to adopt.

"No, these boys weren't the kind to cause trouble at all. They'd come in and have some grub they hadn't had to cook for themselves, and they'd have a few drinks. I never saw any of them worse than what you might call tipsy, an' even then they weren't loud or unpleasant about it. Just got a little bit happier. They were always joking and cutting up amongst themselves anyway, but liquored or cold sober they weren't mean about it. Never heard them make any jokes at the expense of any of the locals. Never looked down on anybody else, if you know what I mean."

Again Longarm nodded. It had been one of the many questions in his mind. It had occurred to him that a group of intelligent and probably fairly well-off Eastern boys coming out here for a summer's work and a summer's romp could create enmity among the locals if they put on airs or thought they were superior to a bunch of cow-smelling local lads. So much for that stillborn theory.

"Any fights that you know of?" he asked.

Race shook his head. "Not a one that I heard of."

"Girl friends?"

"All four of them, Marshal? They were all four killed, you know."

"It wouldn't take but one problem," Longarm reminded him. "If they were all together at the time, the killer could have been after just one but had to kill all four to keep from being discovered and reported by the others."

Race grunted and took another bite of the rich stew. He seemed reluctant to answer that particular question. After a moment he said, "Nothing serious."

"One of them was sparking Emmaline Logan," Longarm said softly.

The young deputy looked surprised. "How long did you say you'd been in town?"

Longarm grinned at him.

Jacob Faust arrived with Longarm's plate of steak and potatoes. He set them down and hurried away, and Longarm sorted out the jumble of tableware that had been delivered with them. He attacked the tallow-fried steak with pleasure.

"Like I said, Longarm, it wasn't anything serious.'

"I had a talk with Miss Logan this afternoon," Longarm said. "She gave me a couple names to check out. An Alfred Wicks . . ."

Race chuckled. "Poor Al. Go ahead an' check on him, of course, but you won't find anything there. Poor Al is so dumb he wouldn't be able to figure out that he should kill the other three too. And I'm not saying that to be unkind. It's just that Alfred isn't quite all there in the brains department. 'Bout two coils short of being able to form a loop, if you know what I mean. But not a mean bone in him. It's true enough that he's smitten with Linny an' he's too dumb to know he doesn't have a chance, but I don't think he could be a good suspect. Lordy," Race laughed, "I never would have thought of poor old Al as a suspect."

"There was one other name," Longarm said. "Hor—" Realization struck him, and he automatically clamped his jaw shut.

He had not made the connection before, when Jacob Faust brought him over here and performed the introductions. Deputy sheriff Race Glesson was *Horace* Glesson.

That was the second name Emmaline Logan had given him.

"Horace Glesson," Race finished for him.

"Well . . . yes."

A hint of sadness flickered in Race's gray eyes. The fact that the girl had named him as a possible suspect must have hurt. But he was man enough, and lawman enough, to stand up to the implied accusation. "I won't be much help to you with that part of your investigation, Marshal."

"Sorry, Race. It just hadn't occurred to me until I started to say it."

The young deputy sighed and laid his spoon aside. "It's logical, of course. I guess I'm no better off than poor Al when it comes to being smitten by Linny." He sighed again. "Lordy, but a man ought to know better. I mean, she's so damn pretty a man just can't think straight when she's around. I know better, of course. She's got notions about city lights and grand balls and a husband who can keep her supplied with the best of everything. Hell, I *know* that. But every time I see her, I forget all my good intentions and get all weak in the knees all over again. I know good an' well I got no business hoping she'll ever come around an' consent to be the wife of a county deputy. I *know* that. But it doesn't do me any good."

Longarm felt sorry for the young man. Not so sorry that he was going to rule Glesson out as a suspect, of course, but definitely sympathetic.

He also felt there was scant probability that Deputy Race Glesson was the murderer he wanted. Still, it would have to be checked out.

The two men finished their meal in a silence that had now become awkward, and when he was done Longarm excused himself. "I have to go find a room for the night," he said. "Then I'll probably check the saloon before I turn in. I'll see you there, more'n likely."

"If you don't," Glesson said, "I'll meet you here for breakfast, and we can ride out to where the bodies were found. Jacob opens at six, if that's all right with you."

"Fine," Longarm said. He paid for his meal, collected his gear from behind Faust's counter, and went in search of a rooming house, since Peyton did not seem to have a hotel.

Chapter 7

The rooming house was shabby but seemed cleaner than the other offerings available. It was run by an aging widow who told him in entirely too much detail about her railroading husband who had been killed in a winter derailment on the Kansas plains. By the time Longarm was able to get his things situated in the small room and disengage himself from the lady, he knew much more than he cared to about the infinite virtues of F. Anderson Rurick. After spending so much time looking at the tightly prim and much-wrinkled lips of the Widow Rurick, Longarm could not help but wonder if Mr. Rurick's many virtues had only been recognized *after* that gentleman's demise.

But he was being highly critical, he reminded himself, and possibly unkind as well. He finally succeeded in excusing himself with some degree of politeness and walked back to the small business district of Peyton. The bay mare was comfortably settled in Mrs. Rurick's shed with a fresh bait of grain, and it hardly seemed worth the bother to saddle her again for a trip of only a few hundred yards.

The town's single saloon was on the same side of the main street as Jacob Faust's restaurant and was the easternmost of the several businesses. There was an open gap between it and the barbershop, put there not from any conscious effort to separate the saloon from the "respectable" businesses of the community, obviously, but by accident. The now-vacant lot between the two structures showed the remains of a building which had burned down on that site, probably within the past year. The roofs and side walls of the adjoining buildings gave evidence of repairs since their original construction, and Longarm guessed that the owners of those businesses would have the railroad's water tank and the ample supply of well water in this area to thank for the salvation of their businesses.

The saloon turned out to be homey and friendly, the kind of place a man could patronize for relaxation and conversation rather than hell-raising. The beer was served in heavy glass mugs, the backbar wall was liberally decorated with mirrors, and the many lamps in use all had tempered glass globes to protect the flames from disturbance. Any place with all that much expensively breakable equipment, Longarm knew, would not have a reputation for rowdiness.

Longarm noticed, too, that while there were a few card games in progress at the tables, there was no display of gaming equipment, no wheel of fortune or roulette table.

All in all, he thought, a friendly sort of place.

He did not, however, see any faces that were already friendly to him. Neither Jacob Faust nor Race Glesson was in the place, and the only person he recognized among the several dozen customers was the blacksmith. The smith was sitting at a brown-felt-covered table with several prosperous looking men dressed for riding. When Longarm entered, the man leaned forward and said something to his companions, but otherwise ignored the tall federal man.

"I don't suppose you'd have some Maryland rye on hand?" Longarm asked the bartender without much hope. Small saloons in small towns rarely carried his favorite tipple, a fact which rankled but which he had long since learned to accept.

The barman smiled. "Would you care to place a wager on that, sir?"

Longarm's tanned face creased in a broad smile. "No, but I'll certainly thank you if you could pour me a shot or two."

The man rummaged under the bar for a moment and produced a bottle from which he had to wipe a considerable amount of dust before he could uncork it. He poured and Longarm thanked him.

"You're the U. S. marshal, aren't you?" the bartender asked as he accepted payment for the rye whiskey.

Longarm nodded. "Word does get around, I see." He decided it was not worth the bother to correct the man's slight error of title; very few civilians cared about the distinction between marshal and deputy, in any event.

"Yeah, well, you know how it is."

"Sure. I suppose you knew the dead boys?"

The bartender shrugged. "Not well. I think they were only in here once."

"Really? I thought they liked to come in once or twice a week to have a few drinks."

"Prob'ly they did, but I think they stopped here only the once. Couldn't say that I got to know any of them, you see."

"But this is the only saloon in town, right?" The man's casually offered statement seemed very much in conflict with what Longarm had already been told. And conflicting statements always aroused Longarm's interest far beyond the casual.

"*In* town, I reckon you could say it is, since I'm right downtown, so to speak. As for it being the only place . . . well, I only wisht it was, Marshal. My business'd be a lot better if that was so."

"There's another, then?"

"Yep. Half a mile east on the old wagon road. Place useta be a stage stop. Now it's a hog ranch. An abomination too, if you ask me." The barkeep pursed his lips and shook his head. "Wicked folks there, if you ask me." It seemed not to occur to him that he had, in fact, not been asked.

"Is that where the boys from the survey crew did their drinking?" Longarm asked.

"Wouldn't know," the barman said. "I make it a point not to know what goes on in a den of corruption like that one is. Wickedness, you see. I don't allow wickedness here."

"I see."

"I s'pose now you'll be taking your trade there," the bartender said glumly.

"Only in the line of duty," Longarm soothed. "For my social drinking, you can be sure I'll come here."

The man grunted. He did not show it, but Longarm thought he was pleased.

Longarm took his time enjoying the aged rye and left the carefully non-wicked saloon without ordering another.

A half-mile hike would have been unthinkable for a cowhand, but Longarm quite frankly enjoyed walking. The evening was cool and pleasant, the first stars of the falling night just now appearing in the eastern sky, so he decided to walk out to the hog ranch. The old wagon road, he assumed, was an extension of the east-west road that paralleled the railroad tracks through Peyton, so he started east on foot, swinging his arms briskly and feeling the clean, fresh bite of the plains air deep in his lungs. It was fully dark by the time he reached the saloon where the dead boys must have done their drinking.

The difference between the two watering holes was apparent even before Longarm went inside.

The street near the saloon in town had been lined with wagons and a few saddle horses, and judging by the number of customers who had been inside, Longarm guessed that most of the first place's patrons were townspeople who walked there after work and then walked on to their homes.

Here, at the hog ranch just beyond the edge of town, there was only a single wagon parked outside, but an adjacent corral was full of saddled horses, and a great many more saddled animals had been tied to the outside of the corral rails.

The sounds of piano music and yelping laughter greeted Longarm before he reached the open doorway. This was definitely a livelier spot than the first had been.

Longarm stepped inside. He had no difficulty adjusting his vision here, because very few lamps were in use, and none of those had globes around them. There was not a mirror in sight behind the bar or anywhere else, and the drinks, even whiskey, were being served in tin cups of various sizes.

He could see immediately what the other saloon proprietor had referred to when he spoke about abominations. Milling about among the many customers of the hog ranch were half a dozen hard-faced girls with rice-powdered faces and dresses short enough to expose their calves as well as their ankles.

Off to the right in a corner of the two-story log building there was a tall, gaudily painted wheel of fortune and a small grouping of semicircular tables covered with green felt and marked out for twenty-one and monte.

The trade here was brisk, the customers gleefully loud. Longarm shouldered his way through the crowd and found a more or less empty place at the long, unpolished bar.

"Yeah?"

"Maryland rye," Longarm said.

The barman, who was large enough to do his own bouncing if need be, shook his head. "Barrel whiskey or beer, mister."

"Beer, then." Longarm had had too much experience with the uncertainties of barrel whiskey to deliberately put any of the unknown stuff into his stomach. Gunpowder and tobacco juice were often among the more palatable ingredients in a barrel of bar whiskey.

The man gave him a mug of beer that was at least half head and demanded a dime.

"Mighty proud of your product, aren't you?" Longarm could not resist remarking.

"If you don't want it, get the hell out." So much for any notion that the customer was always right.

Longarm smiled at him and raised the tin mug in a mocking salute. He turned to look around. In spite of the outrageous prices, everyone seemed to be having a thoroughly good time.

A woman who could have passed for twenty at a distance of ten paces in the dim light but whose age doubled when she came nearer sidled over to Longarm and hooked an arm around his waist.

"Hi, honey. Buy me a drink?"

Longarm smiled and shook his head.

She pouted. Her expression was probably intended to convey deep regret and a lingering sweetness. Longarm's reaction was only a mild concern that all of that makeup was going to crack and fall off the aging whore's face.

"Bet I know what you'd really like, honey," the whore persisted. "We could have us a real fine party upstairs." Her hand drifted south and she lightly played with Longarm's butt. "Just the two of us."

Again Longarm smiled and shook his head. He took a swallow of the beer and made a face. If the beer was any indication of the quality of the beverages here, he was damned glad he hadn't ordered the whiskey. The stuff had a sour, greenish flavor that did not sit well on his tongue after the good rye he had just had back in town.

The whore's expression did not change. She beckoned to him with a finger and whispered, "Lean down here a sec, honey."

Longarm did as he was asked, bending so she could whisper into his ear.

"Fuck you, buster."

Longarm straightened. He smiled benignly down into her powdered face. "I wish you well too."

He expected anger. Instead she laughed and, with a shrug, turned and approached another man farther down the bar. After a moment she led the fellow toward the staircase in the back left corner of the place.

Behind him the bartender barked a loud "hey" to get his attention and said, "You're ready for another beer."

"No thanks. I still have plenty."

"Mister, I said you're ready for another beer. That'll be a dime again."

Longarm turned and smiled at him. "I still have plenty, thanks. But I could use a few minutes of your time."

"You weren't listening, bud."

"Oh, I think I was," Longarm said mildly. "And what I think I might do is close this place for a little while. Check on the identities of all your customers. See if any of them are on wanted lists. Something like that."

The belligerent set of the bartender's jaw softened. "What?"

Longarm pulled his wallet out and flipped it open to expose his badge.

"You wouldn't wanta do a thing like that now, would you?" the bartender asked.

Longarm shrugged and smiled. "Maybe we could start this conversation over," he suggested. "I have plenty of beer left here and don't need a refill, but I thank you very much for the offer. And I really would appreciate a few minutes of your valuable time. In private."

The bartender gave him an ingratiatingly eager look that said there was nothing he would rather do than help the federal man in any way he possibly could. He motioned for the other barman down the counter to take over and led Longarm out of the noise to a back room where they could talk more easily. The incidental fact that none of the customers in the place would thus be able to hear the bartender talking about them was not entirely lost on Longarm.

"Anything I can do for you, sir, why, you just ask old John Stoat. *Always* glad to help the law. Yes, sir, any way at all."

"I appreciate that, Mr. Stoat. Indeed I do." Longarm began asking his questions.

Chapter 8

Longarm was neither pleased nor unhappy when he left the hog ranch and started back toward town and the prospects of some highly welcome sleep.

He had not had any particular expectations about what he might learn at the place, so he was not greatly disappointed. Investigations were usually like that—much leg-work and many questions. Only rarely did some of it pay off in valuable answers.

This time, as it was more often than not, he could see no particular results from his questioning. Yes, the bartender remembered the boys. No, they had not gotten into any of the many brawls and scraps that took place in such an establishment. Yes, they enjoyed a drink or three when they came. No, they never got really drunk. Yes, they made use of the girls and the upstairs rooms. No, there could have been no possibility of anyone being jealous about that.

That question, in fact, had brought a look of genuine amusement into the bartender's eyes. "Over any of them gals? *C'mon*, Marshal! Not over any o' *them!*" Longarm had been pretty much forced to agree with the man's assessment of his own employees.

Now, on his way back to the bed that waited for him in the Widow Rurick's house, he reflected that so far he had been able to uncover no really good motive for someone to have murdered all four members of that government survey crew.

There had to be one. There always was. But unless the killings had taken place in a quest for Emmaline Logan's favors—which he quite frankly doubted—he could find no hint so far that might lead him to the murderers.

He walked quickly, enjoying the exercise, thinking that on his way back to Mrs. Rurick's he would stop in at the saloon in town and have another nip from that dusty bottle of Maryland rye before going to bed.

He stopped for a moment and fished a cheroot out of his pocket, found a match and thumbed it afire, and bent his head to the small flame cupped inside the protective curl of his hands.

Far off to the left, somewhere beyond the railroad tracks, there was a wink of flame. Longarm only saw its spearpoint of fire out of the corner of his eye.

"*Jesus!*"

Longarm dropped flat against the ground, match and cigar forgotten.

The quick, ugly *thupp* of a bullet whizzing overhead reached his ears, and a moment later there was the sound of a gunshot.

The double-action .44 came swiftly into his hand, but remained silent. The range was impossibly long.

After a minute or so in which Longarm crabbed sideways on the ground to shift his position, he could hear the distant drum of hoofbeats as someone got the hell away from the scene.

Disgusted with himself, Longarm stood up and brushed the dirt from his coat and trousers. He shoved the Colt back into its holster. He did not make any effort to retrieve his cheroot. Smoking, showing a light that could illuminate him as a target, was something he would have to take up as an indoor pastime until he determined who the hell was shooting at him.

He did a little fancy cussing, unhappy with himself for having forgotten his caution to such a dangerous degree, then continued on to Peyton. There was, he realized, no point at all in trying to determine where the rifleman had shot from this time. When he reached the business area he went on past the saloon. He no longer felt like being in anyone else's company, and he did have most of a bottle of rye in his valise.

Longarm came off the bed in a crouch, moving swiftly to blow out the bedside lamp and snatch the Colt from the holster slung on the bedpost.

The knocking at his door, more of a tapping really, sounded softly for the second time.

Longarm slipped to the side in his stocking feet and softly called out, "Come in."

The doorknob turned, but the door did not open. It rattled only slightly against the resistance of the latch, and the pressure was quickly released. That was what Longarm had been wondering. He knew good and well that the latch was set. The force that was applied against a door that was supposed to be unlocked could have been revealing. As it was, it probably meant that his visitor had no unfriendly intentions.

"I can't," a feminine voice whispered.

"Just a minute." Longarm eased forward and unsnapped the lock on the door, then stepped cautiously aside before he announced that it was open now.

He had no idea who his visitor might be. The voice had not been that of Mrs. Rurick. And he could not think of any other female within a great many miles who might have reason to visit him during the night.

The door swung open and Linny Logan stood outlined in the hallway light. She was looking nervously about, as if fearful that someone might see her there.

Still, she hesitated, apparently unwilling to enter the darkened bedroom.

Longarm ignored her for the moment and, Colt still ready in his hand, checked the short hallway to make sure there was no one with her. Only then did he cross the room to find a match and light the lamp. "Come in if you want," he said.

Linny did, shutting and locking the door behind her. She had looked nervous in the hallway. Now she relaxed.

It occurred to Longarm that he was in his drawers, ready for sleep. It occurred to him too that Linny Logan did not seem in the least bit embarrassed or upset by his state of partial undress.

"Was there something you wanted, Miss Logan?" He sat on the edge of the bed—there was no chair in the small room—and shoved the .44 back where it belonged, reached for a cheroot, and lighted it with the flame from the lamp.

The girl smiled. She set her handbag down on the small bureau and unpinned and removed her stylish hat. "Possibly." She was giving him an odd smile. The expression reminded him somehow of that given by an alley cat to an unwary pigeon.

Longarm tilted his head and narrowed his eyes against the curl of smoke rising from his cheroot.

Linny Logan was every bit as handsome a woman as he remembered. She had changed clothing since he saw her last. Now she was wearing a dress made of dark blue velvet with feathered hat and clutch purse to match. The dress had a bustle that was totally unnecessary with a figure like hers. Her blonde hair was still piled in a complicated confection over her exceptionally pretty face.

"When," he asked, "do you intend to let me in on your secret?"

"Secret?"

"Whatever reason it was that brought you here."

She was still smiling. "Isn't that obvious, sir?"

Longarm gnawed on the end of his cigar while he pondered that for a moment. "Nope," he said finally.

"Surely you realize that a lady has, shall we say, limited opportunities for...fulfillment?" She acted like she expected that to explain everything. As far as Longarm was concerned, it did not.

"Linny."

"Yes?"

"What the hell are you talking about?" It was late. He was tired. He had ridden a long way today, been shot at, and accomplished damn little. If this young woman wanted to come along now and play a bunch of damn games in the middle of the night, she was just going to have to find another player.

Her eyes widened. Then she laughed. "My dear Marshal Long! And I thought you were a rather bright man."

"Only when I'm awake," he said.

She laughed again. "You must understand, sir, that a lady of quality requires discretion. Local boys talk too much. Passing gentlemen of quality are rare. And they must be cultivated with care, don't you see." She sat on the far end of the bed and began stripping her gloves off, then bent over to begin unbuttoning the ankle-high tops of her dainty shoes.

"Is that supposed to explain something?"

"But of course it does." She kicked off first one shoe and then the other. She began removing pins from her hair, allowing it to fall slowly into a cascade that spilled across her shoulders and down her back. "You seem quite clean, don't you see. Almost a gentleman. Lord knows you are physically attractive enough. Muscular and quite slim. That is very important, you know. I abhor fat men." She faked a slight shudder, then laughed. "So quite probably fate will require me to marry a fat man. A *rich* fat man, to be sure, but just you wait and see." She laughed again, and shifted position so that her back was toward him. "Would you mind?"

"Mind what?"

"My buttons, silly. Surely you don't think I can manage them by myself."

It crossed Longarm's mind that he quite probably should become stuffy and brave about the whole thing. Refuse the girl's request. Send her packing after the spanking he had more or less promised her earlier. After all, a very nice young deputy sheriff had as much as declared this girl to be his intended, and there is such a thing as loyalty among law officers.

On the other hand, a youngster with Race Glesson's limited prospects was not exactly likely to gather in this particular prize. And if he ever did, the poor sap was going to find that his prize was worth a damn sight less than he suspected. So loyalty to a brother peace officer should hardly enter into the equation.

There was also the disquieting fact that Miss Logan's approach was not entirely complimentary. Clean, was he? *Almost* a gentleman. Not local. Probably discreet. Not fat. When he thought about it, Longarm had judged beef on the hoof with more sensitivity and compassion than Miss Logan was now showing.

Still . . . he started at the back of her neck, flipping buttons out of their holes with nimble, practiced fingers.

"Thank you." She stood up, slipped the dress from her shoulders, and stepped out of it. She sat back down and stripped her stockings down long, admirably shapely legs. She turned to enjoy the effect this display should be having on her audience of one.

Longarm feigned boredom and peered at the stack of ash that was building on the end of his cheroot.

Emmaline Logan made a face, a pretty parody of a pout. She stood and struck a pose, wearing only her chemise and drawers. She had no need for a corset.

Longarm grinned at her.

Apparently that was enough. Moving slowly, obviously very much aware that she was being watched now, the girl pulled her chemise over her head and dropped it onto the floor. She stepped out of her drawers and stood naked in front of him. She turned, giving him ample opportunity to see everything she had to offer.

It was, he admitted, quite a bundle. Her breasts were full and ripe and firm, standing proudly away from her rib cage with large, pointy, hard nipples.

Her waist was tiny, her hips full. Her complexion was smooth and creamy, her pubic hair a thick, golden muff of curls already moist.

With a confidence that bordered on arrogance—no, he decided; it didn't border, damn it; it traveled far across any borderlines and *was* arrogant as hell—she approached him and stood with her head held haughtily back and her gorgeous legs braced wide apart so that the wet lips of her sex were immediately in front of him as he sat on the edge of the bed.

"Do you like what you see, Marshal?" she asked in a husky voice.

Longarm shrugged. "Sure." He flicked the ash from his cigar and took another puff on it.

"I like it best when a man licks me, Marshal. I like it when he gets down on his knees and licks my pussy."

"Do you, now?"

"Oh, yes." Her voice was becoming low and throaty as she prepared herself for what she knew was to come. "That is what I like, Marshal. Do it. Do it now. Lick me there." She reached out and cupped the back of his head with a perfectly manicured hand. She pulled him down and forward.

She canted her hips forward and raised one shapely foot to prop beside him on the bed. The lips of her sex gaped wider, tantalizing, demanding, already soaked with the moisture of her feverish readiness.

Her eyes widened. She could scarcely believe what was happening.

Instead of dropping to his knees and eating her, as she demanded, Custis Long resisted the pressure of her hand.

He looked up into her eyes and laughed.

"But..."

Longarm laid his cheroot aside. "Don't worry about it, Linny. You aren't making me mad. Not quite. Perverse, yes, but not mad."

"But..."

"But *everybody always* jumps when little Linny says she wants to get laid? Is that it? Sure it is. Well, Linny . . . surprise, surprise. Not everybody's going to roll over and bark when you say they ought to. That's something you'd better learn, Linny. Better you learn it now than when it's too late."

"But . . ."

"Shhh."

Normally a gentle and considerate man, as concerned with his partner's pleasure as with his own, Longarm deliberately laughed again. Instead of dropping to his knees and playing the faithful hound for this arrogant, unfeeling wench, he stood, towering far above her.

She looked unsure of herself now, almost frightened. "But . . ."

"Shut up."

He took her by the upper arm and levered her down onto the bed. Her eyes were very wide. And he noticed that she landed—and remained—with her exquisite legs wide apart.

"This isn't what I planned."

"Good," he said. He shucked out of his drawers and leaned over her.

If her eyes had been wide with surprise before, they were fit to burst out of their sockets now. "I don't think I can take all that." She was staring at him. She licked her dry lips.

"All right," he said calmly. He turned away and bent to retrieve his drawers.

"But . . ."

"You said you couldn't take it all, didn't you? Well, I don't want to hurt you. Don't want to play games, either, for that matter. So . . . if you've changed your mind, you've changed it. Get dressed and go home." He reached for his cigar.

"Damn you." She grabbed up the nearest thing at hand—fortunately, a pillow—and hurled it at him.

Longarm laughed. "Careful, Linny. Keep this up and you might make me mad. I might spank you yet."

"Oh, God." She wilted in a breathless surge of eager passion. "Would you?"

"What?"

"Spank me. Please." She rolled off the bed onto her knees. She crept to him and bent to kiss his feet, licking frantically between his toes and up the strong columns of his leg to the smaller but equally strong column of his cock. She gobbled him noisily if with little expertise.

He reached under her arms, her globular breasts pressing warmly against his wrists, and lifted her to her feet. She immediately attacked his chest with wet, slurping licks and kisses. "Spank me, please."

"Later," he said.

"Promise. You have to promise."

"We'll see."

She was trying to wrap herself around his waist, lifting and reaching, working desperately to impale herself on his stiff rod of heated flesh. "Please. Please."

Perversity and stoicism have their limits. Longarm leaned forward, pressing her back onto the bed under him. He covered her body with his and plunged deep inside her with a swift, sure rush.

Linny moaned and clutched at him with arms, legs, and lips alike. She clung to him with a leechlike ferocity and began to bang her hips against him with a mad abandon. She squealed and groaned and whimpered, writhed and thrust again and again. Longarm braced himself stiff and unmoving above her, letting her do the work for both of them, taking the wild, wild ride she offered.

It was, he thought, a damned strange performance from a damned strange girl.

But he did not feel like arguing. After all, he was almost a gentleman. The least he could do would be to act almost like one.

Chapter 9

Longarm felt a trifle sorry for Race Glesson when the two of them rode out about six-thirty the next morning. The young deputy had pledged his heart to a woman who would never be his wife and a woman who would make no man a good wife. A good lay, yes—but a good wife, never.

It did not make matters any better that Glesson insisted on talking about Emmaline Logan for nearly the entire trip, exclaiming over her undeniable beauty and, even harder for Longarm to take, admiring as well her virtue in rejecting all social contact from among her local suitors. The young man must surely have been aware that any woman of genuine value could not be the admitted gold digger that Linny Logan was. But if that simple fact had ever pierced Glesson's emotion-colored awareness, he did not admit it to his traveling companion.

"Mark my words, Longarm, I'm going to win out in the end. I'm determined to show her the stuff I'm made of.

True love, after all, must surely prevail."

Longarm grunted, only half hearing what the sheriff's deputy was saying. His attention was locked on the skyline, shifting over every fold and swale they passed as they rode. Whoever it was who was trying to shoot him, and for whatever reason, luck would only carry him so far. From now on, vigilance would have to be the price of survival.

"Hey."

"What?" Longarm eased back on the reins and the little mare slowed. He had not really been paying attention to Glesson. Now he realized that the deputy had turned his horse aside at a slight angle and was waiting for Longarm to join him.

"I said the place we want is over here."

Longarm stood in his stirrups and looked around. To the uninitiated, it would seem almost impossible to distinguish this one particular spot from any other on the gently rolling, baked-dry plains around them. But over there was a dry wash with a peculiar, distinctive shape to its undercut bank. And here was a patch of soapweed growing in the lee of a small red boulder that looked very much out of place on the bare, sparsely grassed soil.

"Sorry," Longarm said. "Reckon I was wandering."

"In more ways than one, I'd say."

"Yeah." Longarm rubbed his eyes. "Not much sleep last night."

Glesson looked sympathetically concerned. "I know how that can be," he said. "I never sleep well in a strange bed either. Better rolled up in a blanket out of doors than trying to sleep somewhere new."

Longarm grunted something that could have been taken for agreement, but in truth the quickly offered expression of caring made him feel like something of a bastard. After

70

all, it was the girl Race Glesson loved who had kept him up to all hours of the night. Damned if that wasn't making Longarm feel like something of a traitor, even if the poor fellow did have no claims he could reasonably make on the girl. And it certainly was not that Long had forced his attentions on her. Far from that. Still...

He rubbed his eyes again and kneed the bay in behind Glesson's tall roan gelding.

"Just over this rise," Race was saying. "They'd already been messed with some by the time I got here, of course. A rider for the Three Bar Seven found them. He turned them all over, making sure there wasn't anybody still breathing or anything, and I kind of get the idea he might have checked their pockets too before he came in to report the deaths."

"Why do you say that?"

"They were all college boys, probably all of them fairly well off. I mean, they were out here as much for a lark as for a job. But when I inventoried their stuff to send back to their folks, I found between a dollar and a half and two dollars and a quarter in each of them's pockets. Aside from being too little, I'd say that it was too pat, too much of a coincidence that all of them would've been carrying so close to the same amount. So the way I figure it, this cowboy decided that was a likely amount for a man to have in his pockets, an' made sure he left that there when he put the rest of their cash in his own poke."

"I'd say you're likely right," Longarm agreed. He nudged the bay up beside the younger man and encouraged him with the added comment, "A lot of deputies I've known would fall for it. You think things through pretty good."

The compliment earned him a grin of genuine pleasure. "Thanks."

"No need to thank somebody for something you've honestly earned."

They topped the rise and stopped, looking down into a basin so shallow it was difficult to detect.

"The wagon was there," Race said, pointing. "The beds were between it and the fire. You can still see where the fire was built. The wagon tracks running down over there —I made them myself when I hauled the bodies to town. They'd started to the west of us an' were working their way east. You might still can see the marks the iron tires cut in the ground. Over there, they'd be."

"Horses?" Longarm asked.

"Hobbled. Time I got here they'd strayed about a mile. I choused them in an' used them to draw the wagon with the bodies."

"What about the equipment?"

"It wasn't tampered with the least bit that I could tell. Of course, I didn't know what was in the wagon to begin with, but there sure wasn't any signs of anything being missing. Everything you'd expect was there. Transit an' sticks an' chains an' such. Along with the personal gear like clothes and razors. No, far as I could make out, none of it was messed with."

Longarm grunted. He sat and pulled out a cheroot, lighting it and drawing on it slowly while he surveyed the murder scene, trying to bring it to life in his mind's eye.

"Any tracks left by the killers?"

"A few smudges. Nothing you could call a print. Course, that's about all you can expect on this ground. It bakes dry as 'dobe and won't hold a track worth a shit. What little I could see, I'd say they come in from the west, over there, and rode right up to the sleeping camp. Sat on horseback right over top of them and fired down into the bodies before the boys ever woke up."

The tall federal deputy grunted again and sucked on his cigar. "Empty shells?"

"Plenty. I've got them back at my place, if you want to see them. Not that they'll tell you much. Plain old brass shells like you can reload a hundred times and buy just damn near anyplace you can buy shotshells. Ten-gauge, but that doesn't mean anything around here. This isn't what you'd call a shotgunner's country. Not for sport. The boys as carry them will do it for close-in defense—better than a pistol any day, and easier to handle when you're in a fight —or use the same size for hunting waterfowl for the table. Which you intend to do, you can tell by the length of the barrel. Short for fighting, long for ducks and geese."

Longarm had not particularly needed the lecture—he was rather well versed in fighting and firearms himself—but he did not point that out to the youngster. That would only have embarrassed the boy and would have served no purpose except to make Longarm out to be the big shot, which would hardly have been a useful purpose.

"Do you happen to recall how many there were?" he asked.

"How many what?"

"Empty shells."

"Oh. Let me think a minute. Ten. Yeah, I'm sure of it. There were ten of them. Does that mean anything?"

Longarm shrugged. "I'll tell you for sure when we get these yahoos. It *could* mean they were using double-barrel shotguns, since it's an even number. Could mean there were five of them using double-barrel guns. But then it could as easy mean it was one lone, mean bastard with a single-barrel gun who only had ten shells in his pocket and meant to use them all. Damned if I could tell just now, but it's the sort of thing to keep in mind just in case the information comes in handy sometime."

"It wasn't any lone man with a single-barrel or even a double-barrel gun," Glesson said positively.

"Why is that?"

"There wasn't a one of them moved off his bed. An' I'd suspect that a ten-bore gun firing down over top of you at night would get your attention plenty quick. I'd have to say at the very least there was two men with double-barrel guns. There might have been more, but there was at least that many."

Longarm thought about that for a moment, mentally going through the motions of *being* a lone man with a shotgun and a mad on for those four sleeping boys.

He imagined himself standing over them, cocking his hammer—or hammers—then triggering his shots into the sleeping bodies, twisting the thumb lever and breaking the shotgun open, reloading with fresh shells already palmed in his left hand and held behind the fore end.

No, he concluded, there was no way one man could have handled it by himself. Not without at least one and probably two of his victims coming up off their blankets to fight or to flee or if nothing else to stand there in dumb amazement while the killer continued the work of cutting them down.

If they were all still in their blankets, they had to have been killed by more than one man.

"You're right again," Longarm said finally. "At least two. Possibly more. No idea from the tracks?"

Glesson shook his head. "Not enough to go on. I couldn't even tell which of the smudges were made by the boys' own horses and which by the cowboy who found them. No way at all to take a tally on how many there would have been in the killing party. Hell, they were bedded right beside the wagon, practically. Their own horses had been there some too, beforehand."

"Uh-huh." Longarm took a final pull on his cheroot and raised a boot heel out of his stirrup to grind the coal out before he dropped it into the grass. The country was dry now, and no sensible man would want to take a chance on starting a grass fire.

"Did you follow the wagon tracks back any distance to see where they'd been that day?" he asked.

"No. Did what I could here an' figured I'd better get them in and on the train so they could get some embalming while it'd still do some good."

He did not need to explain any further. Longarm knew as well as Race Glesson did just how quickly a body could start to bloat and decay in the hot weather they had been having lately. And it was at least possible that one of the dead boys' families would want to open the coffin when those bodies were delivered back to the grieving parents.

"I think we should do that if you don't mind," Longarm suggested. He did not bother to mention that he would backtrack the survey wagon himself whether the local deputy wanted to go along or not.

"Whatever you think," Race agreed.

Longarm did not bother, either, to approach any nearer to the site of the murders. Glesson's description was good enough for that. Instead he walked the bay forward until he could make out the first faint marks made by iron-tired wheels and followed them toward the west, back in the direction the survey crew had been coming from on that last evening of their short lives.

The tracks wandered in an apparently willy-nilly pattern for several miles. They twisted and turned in no obvious plan or order, though there must have been some reason for it all.

Probably, Longarm decided, they were taking the wagon

of equipment directly along the route they had been surveying. Longarm would have expected them to drive the wagon in a more direct route and use their mapping pens to outline the route on paper. But maybe for convenience or laziness or whatever other reason, they instead took the wagon along the exact line of the survey. Certainly they had that choice here, where nearly all of the sprawling country could be easily traversed by a wagon.

They rode westward for several miles, moving very slowly and studying the ground. The only thing they found along the route was a pair of cigarette butts at one point. The cigarettes had been thrown down and allowed to burn themselves out instead of being crushed out. That almost certainly meant they were dropped there by the boys in the survey crew, Longarm thought, because a Westerner would have known better. At least any plainsman who had ever seen a grass fire would have known better.

After about three miles of slow, unproductive travel, Longarm pulled the mare to a halt and turned in his saddle to look back the way they had come.

"Have you noticed the holes we've been passing?"

"What holes?" Obviously Glesson had not noticed them.

"Over here. Been one like this every little way. Not spaced regular, but every so often." Longarm swung down off the bay and led her over to the small hole in the hard soil. He hunkered down to examine it more closely, and Race joined him.

"What do you make of that?" Longarm asked.

"Damned if I know."

Longarm grunted. "That's two of us."

The hole was small, an inch by approximately an inch and a half, and its corners were squared. It could have been caused by no animal—not with square corners—and it extended only a few inches into the sun-baked soil.

"Strange," Longarm said.

"Could have been left from the last rains, I suppose," Glesson said. "Somebody could have poked the ground with a stick, a walking stick or something, and it dried that way."

"Maybe."

So-called freshness of sign had no bearing here, Longarm knew. A mark could be made in the ground after a rain and still be there years later, after the sun had had time to dry the disturbed soil into a natural adobe. Hell, he had seen places not too terribly far away where there were tracks left by an animal no living human had ever laid eyes on, animals that would have to have been so big they would make the biggest circus elephant look small beside them. So Race's suggestion was not beyond the possible or even past the probable.

Still, the marks were more or less along the line of travel the survey wagon had taken, and there were a number of them.

"Survey stakes?" Longarm suggested. It was the only halfway logical thing he could think of.

"They were out here to map, not stake, weren't they?"

Longarm sighed. "Yeah. Damn curious, though. Maybe there's other holes *off* the line of travel. We've only been riding along the wagon tracks, after all. If there are other holes like this poked all around, somebody hunting for something or dowsing for a well or whatever, we wouldn't have seen them."

"We'll take a look."

They remounted and left the route the survey wagon had taken, but they could find no more of the small, square-cornered holes.

"Maybe we're just missing them?" Glesson hazarded.

"Maybe," Longarm said skeptically. He did not believe it, and he doubted that Glesson did either. "Hell, let's go back and see what Jacob has for lunch."

"Whatever suits you."

They turned their horses south and Race led the way unerringly to the north edge of Peyton.

Chapter 10

The bullet whipped across just in front of Longarm's saddle. He heard it pass, heard the dull, meaty *thwack* as it struck living flesh, and soon afterward heard the hollow bark of the muzzle report. By that time Longarm was on the ground, the little bay mare between him and the source of the gunshot.

He snatched his Winchester from the scabbard and laid it over the saddle, using the polished leather of the McClellan for a rest.

For a change, he was able to see exactly where the shot had come from.

They had already reached the northern limits of Peyton. Perhaps three hundred yards east of where they now were stood the tumbledown remains of an old dugout that must have housed one of the area's earliest settlers. The dugout had fallen into disuse, and right now, immediately above it, Longarm could see a faint wisp of smoke hanging in the motionless midday air.

"You son of a bitch," Longarm muttered. He thumbed back the hammer of the always loaded and ready Winchester and let a slug fly toward the spot from which the shot had come.

Wood splintered from one of the roof beams resting at the ground level of the dugout. The range was too long for pinpoint accuracy, but Longarm could still make some fur fly and hope for luck to connect him with his intended target. He levered another round into the chamber of the Winchester and dusted the dugout again, repeating the sequence of deadly activity until the rifle was empty, its barrel hot.

That he had accomplished nothing with all that noise was quickly evident. The dugout had been deep enough to hide a horse, because now the distant figure of a man could be seen. The man mounted, turned in his saddle to throw a luck shot in Longarm's direction—wherever it went, it was not close enough to be heard or worried about—and raced away.

"Bastard," Longarm muttered. The man obviously knew what kind of rifle Longarm carried. He must have counted the deputy's shots until the Winchester was empty, then knew he would be safe to make his break.

Safe, though, only if he could outrun the bay mare.

"Come on, Race." Longarm shoved the empty Winchester back into its boot and swung quickly onto the mare. "Let's run the bastard down."

There was no response from his right. Come to think of it, he realized, there had been no firing from Race Glesson's position either.

Longarm checked the mare from the jump she had been ready to make and swung her back toward Glesson.

The young deputy was face down on the ground beside his standing horse.

There was a pool of gaudy scarlet beside and beneath him. He had lost a huge quantity of blood.

"Shit!" Longarm murmured.

Glesson moved his head weakly, motioning Longarm to give chase to the ambusher. The kid was down, but he was still game. His lips formed the word "go," but no sound came out.

Longarm turned his head to look with bitter but useless fury toward the disappearing figure of the racing horseman. If he gave chase now, there was a slim possibility that he might be able to catch the ambusher. But if he left Race Glesson lying here untended, there was a virtual certainty that Glesson would die from loss of blood. He had already lost too much.

Longarm dismounted again, ignoring the rifleman who was escaping. Muttering curses and the vilest of threats, he knelt beside the county deputy.

The slug had torn a gaping wound in Race's left thigh after it passed in front of Longarm. That had been the sound of impact Longarm heard.

The wound was large and ragged and was bleeding entirely too freely.

Longarm snatched Race's bandanna from around the young man's neck and knotted it around his thigh above the bullet wound. He used the haft of the youngster's belt knife to twist the cloth and tighten it into a tourniquet, slowing and eventually stopping the flow of blood from the wound.

Longarm looked up. People were beginning to approach now, although with caution.

"You," Longarm called, pointing to the nearest of several men in the gathering crowd. "Fetch a wagon, man."

The man hesitated.

"Now!"

He turned and scuttled away in an awkward lope.

"You, ma'am—bring me a blanket to wrap him in."

The woman nodded and hurried off. She was back with a blanket moments before the man arrived with a springboard wagon.

With the help of several others from the group of curious townspeople, who became more helpful when they saw who it was who had been hurt, Longarm wrapped Glesson in the blanket and lifted him gently into the back of the wagon.

"Do you have a doctor in town?"

One of the men shook his head. "Got the barber. Barber surgeon, he is."

Longarm nodded. A barber surgeon knew as much as most doctors about cuts and burns and external wounds. More than some. "Let's go. But slow now. Let's be careful with him."

Glesson by now had passed out from the combined shock and pain. Mercifully, he was unable to feel the jostling and bouncing of the light wagon as it transported him as gently as possible into the town and around to the barbershop.

"Harry!" someone called as they got closer. "Hurry up! It's young Race 'as been shot."

The barber, a plump man wearing a sleeved white apron over his clothes, dashed out onto the boardwalk in front of his establishment.

He took charge immediately. "Get aside now. Damn it, boys, give me room to work here. Oh, sorry, Ella. Din' see you there. Come on, boys, move aside. That's better."

He turned. "Give me a knife, Tom. Thanks." He opened the clasp knife and used it to slice away the cloth that partially covered the wound.

The entry hole was bad enough. The exit wound was awful indeed. It looked big enough to hide a guinea egg and was pulsing redly with seepage from the torn flesh. The barber grunted to himself and leaned closer to adjust his glasses and peer at the damage that had been done.

"Filthy damn hole," he muttered. "Threads shoved all the way back here. Gonna have to run an alcohol soak all the way through or it'll fester. Gotta have help holding him down. You, Tom, and you, mister, carry him in. The rest o' you boys stay close. We'll all be needed to hold him still."

Longarm ducked away before he might be assigned one of the chores of helping.

Not that he did not want to help Race Glesson keep his leg. Far from it. But the barber seemed to have that matter well in hand. Much better, in fact, than Longarm could have done. All he needed here was some unskilled labor to help hold his patient immobile. Any of the townspeople could manage that.

In the meantime, a would-be killer was riding merrily away. There was practically no chance that Longarm could catch the ambusher now.

But practically no chance is not quite the same as no chance.

If there was any chance at all, Longarm fully intended to make the most of it. He swung onto the bay and turned her away from the busy, worried crowd in front of the barbershop. He was reloading the Winchester as he rode.

Chapter 11

"How're you feeling, Race?"

The young deputy managed a weak smile, but he looked pale and his face was drawn and tired. It was apparent that he was still in a great deal of pain. Instead of answering Longarm's question, he asked one of his own. "Did you get the son of a bitch?"

Longarm shook his head. "Too much of a start, I'm afraid. Never even found a hint of a track after the first few yards. But at least we have something to go on now."

"What's that?" Glesson's voice was weak too, no more than a whisper. But then, he had lost a great deal of blood.

"The place where his horse was tied down in that hole —you know, in the old dugout—was softer ground, shaded part of the time, I guess, and it probably collects some water in there too when there's some to collect. Anyway, I found some pretty decent prints where the horse was standing. I'll recognize the marks again if I see them."

"Good," Race whispered.

"Is there anything I can get you?"

The young deputy rolled his head slowly from side to side.

"Anyone I should notify?"

Again the slow shake of the head. "Ja..." He coughed, and the abrupt motion twisted his young face with waves of fresh pain.

"Easy, now," Longarm soothed. He took a small tumbler of water from the bedside table and offered it so Glesson could wet his lips with a bird-brief sip of the liquid.

"Thanks." He sighed and seemed to relax somewhat. "Jacob wired the sheriff. Don' have extra men to send. You'll be on your own here, Longarm."

The federal man did not mention that he was used to being on his own and in some ways preferred it. For one thing, damn it, if he had been alone today, Race Glesson would not have been hit by a bullet intended for Custis Long. That fact rankled, and made him all the more determined to find and bring in whoever the bastard was who was so intent on putting a bullet into Billy Vail's deputy.

Instead, Longarm took the worry in Glesson's voice as an opportunity to maybe make the kid feel better. "I don't want to bother you when you need your rest, but if you wouldn't mind I'll likely stop in here from time to time and ask your advice about the way things are here. Would that be too much trouble?"

"Anything I can do, Longarm."

"Thanks." He thought Glesson's voice had been stronger, perhaps a small measure more purposeful, when he said it. If so, that was a good sign. In Longarm's unschooled but practical experience, a man will heal quicker and get back on his feet all the faster if he has some purpose in his life and something to work toward. "Hope you're better soon, Race," he added. "I may be needing your help with this thing."

"Quick as I can," the boy promised.

"Good." Longarm reached for a cheroot, then thought better of the impulse. The smoke might be bothersome to the wounded man. "One thing you could help me with right now," he went on.

"Yes?"

"That cowboy who found the bodies. I'd like to talk with him. I believe the reports said his name is Alvin Kestle. Is that right?"

Race nodded.

"Where could I find him?"

"Three Bar Seven. North an' east. Not so far north as where the boys were murdered. Farther east from there."

Longarm nodded. "Kestle. Three Bar Seven. Got it."

"Longarm?"

"Uh-huh."

"If there's anything else . . ."

Longarm smiled at him. "I'll come and ask you. That's a promise. I mean, you might be flat on your back, but you can still contribute a lot to this investigation. Meantime, I'll also be trying to find out who put that bullet into you."

For the first time, Glesson's eyes came alight with total interest. "You do that," he urged. "That'un I kinda want."

"If I can, Race, I'll damn sure give him to you." He smiled. "With a pretty red ribbon tied round his neck."

"Good."

Longarm said goodbye and let himself out the front door of the Glesson home, where Race had been taken from the barbershop. It was not until he looked the boy up and found him abed in his parents' home that Longarm realized he was a local boy who had been deputized and not a deputy assigned here from elsewhere. That helped explain the townspeople's concern over him, a concern that was not always given when a law officer was in trouble.

Longarm mounted the now tired bay mare and rode her to the shed behind Mrs. Rurick's place. It was much too late in the day by now to set out for the Three Bar Seven, and both he and the horse were long overdue for a bite to eat.

It was well past mid-morning, and Longarm had not yet found the Three Bar Seven. The incomplete directions to the place he had been able to get from the people in town left him unsure of whether he had already come too far or not half far enough. The folks in town depended on the area ranches for trade but apparently rarely visited out in the nearly empty country.

There were no high points in this country where a man could get a really good look at the land around him, but he made do the best he could by finding the highest of the many low rises around him and riding to the top of it.

He could see no buildings in any direction. Peyton and its distinctive water tower landmark had disappeared behind him hours before. But here and there he could make out more or less regular scars on the ground that might have been wagon trails. The problem was, he had no idea which of those might lead to the Three Bar Seven.

Off to the east, four miles or so, he could see a slight, almost misty discoloration against the sere brown backdrop of the rolling land. There might, he thought, be smoke there. Whether the smoke came from a building or a branding fire hardly made any difference, as long as he could ask directions. On the other hand, he could as easily be looking at a haze of dust raised by a herd of cattle or even antelope. Both were fairly thick here. Of the cattle, well over half wore the Three Bar Seven brand, a numeral three stacked above a straight line and below that the numeral seven. The brand was applied in very large figures on the left flank. The size of the brand told Longarm that the owner of the brand was an old-fashioned cowman, possibly one of the earliest users of this country for graze. The modern trend, now that hides were beginning to be worth something, was for brands to be smaller. Generally speaking, the larger the brand, the longer it had been in use.

Longarm turned the mare toward where he had seen the smoke or dust and bumped her into a smooth lope that she seemed both willing and entirely capable of maintaining for mile upon mile.

His first impression, that it was smoke he had seen, turned out to be accurate. He topped the last rise and found a small set of corrals and what looked like a stovepipe rising straight up out of the hillside. A windmill had been erected beside the corrals to feed a stock tank and probably provide household water also. The stovepipe, of course, came not from the hillside, as it looked from the rear, but from the roof of a dugout.

This dugout was very much in use, and when Longarm rode down into the yard between it and the corrals he could see that it was newly built. Dugout houses were neither fashionable nor particularly clean, but they had several distinct advantages. For one thing, they were incredibly cheap. No nails or purchased hardware were necessary for their construction, and they could be built by anyone who owned or could borrow a shovel . . . for that matter, by a patient man with nothing but a pointed stick for a tool and a willingness to drag dead wood for the roof supports. They were effectively insulated by the very earth that formed their walls, cool in the heat of summer and easily warmed even in the most severe of winter's storms. Their disadvantages included mud when it rained, and rodents and bugs in the roof and walls at all times of the year. They were still as practical now, though, as they had been before the railroad made lumber readily available on the plains.

Longarm rode into the yard in front of the door to the dugout. Door was a title offered more by courtesy than description, since it was nothing but a beef hide nailed to the front rafter log overhead. He called out a hello.

His answer was the appearance of a gaping shotgun muzzle shoved out beside the beef-hide door covering.

The muzzle was aimed quite accurately toward Longarm's belt buckle.

Chapter 12

Longarm smiled his most charming and, he hoped, disarm-
ing smile. "Hello," he said in a conversational tone.

Whoever was holding that shotgun on him, he wanted
to give no offense. In the deep shadow of the windowless
interior he could not see who or what was holding the gun.
He could barely make out the earred-back hammers of the
double gun. He kept staring at those hammers rather than
the muzzles. Not that it would make any difference. Once
a hammer started to fall, there would be no time at all for
a man to throw himself aside and escape the pattern of an
open-bored scattergun at this range. No one had reaction
time that quick.

"I was hoping to borrow a drink of water for myself and
the horse here," he said pleasantly.

There was no response. The twin tubes of the shotgun
barrels wavered for a moment, then steadied again.

"Could I step down? Please?"

The muzzles sagged. Unexpectedly, the gun fell. It dropped to the ground and bounced. Longarm winced as he saw one of the cocked hammers jar free from the impact and spring forward.

The hammer fell onto the striking pin with a sharp clack, but there was no bellow of sound accompanying it. The gun had been empty.

The gun fell, and immediately afterward there was the dull thump of a human body falling to the ground. The beefhide door swung back into place, the empty and useless tubes of the empty shotgun showing beneath it.

What the ...

Longarm dropped off the bay mare and hurried across the hard-packed earth of the ranch yard. He held the hide aside and stepped inside the dugout.

There was no lamp or candle burning inside, and he had to drape the hide door aside to get enough light to see.

A woman lay on the earthen floor, the shotgun in front of her. She had fainted or passed out, from what cause Longarm could not guess.

Without taking time to think about it, he bent and scooped her up. She weighed less in his arms than many children he had lifted onto his knee.

The dugout was as good as unfurnished. There was no table, no bed, no chairs. Several wooden crates were doing double service as stools and storage containers. A pallet of blankets had been laid in one corner of the small structure. Instead of a stove there was only a beehive fireplace built against the back wall from native stone mortared with native clay and grass stems. He carried her to the pallet and placed her down as gently as he could.

"Lady? Ma'am?" He examined her as well as he could

without overstepping the bounds of propriety. She was very pale and painfully thin, but seemed not to have any wounds or obvious injuries. He rubbed her cheeks, trying to bring her around. Her skin felt dry and unnaturally warm to the touch, like parchment just taken from a warm oven.

He looked around the place, but there was no water bucket. He took a pan from beside the fireplace and hurried out to the stock tank to dip it into the sun-warmed water there.

Longarm straightened and would have rushed back to the dugout, but a vaguely unpleasant odor halted him. He bent again, leaned closer to the tank, and sniffed. The water had a faintly sour smell, not that of a sulphur well but something else. He could not exactly place the smell, but he knew he did not like it. It smelled unhealthy.

He sniffed the water in the pan to confirm that the odor was in the water, then gingerly tasted it. The liquid had a slightly bitter flavor. He swished it around in his cheeks and spat it back onto the ground, careful to allow none of the suspect fluid to pass his throat.

When he returned to the dugout, he stopped at the mare's side to take down his canteen and carry that inside with him also.

He found a scrap of cloth and dipped it into the pan he had brought in from the stock tank. He suspected that the tank water was tainted somehow, but it would be useful enough for washing purposes or for trying to ease a fever. He bathed the woman's face with the cloth but kept the fluid away from her lips.

"Ma'am?" he asked again.

This time she stirred slightly. It was not much of a response, but he thought it a hopeful sign.

He set the pan aside, uncapped his canteen, and held the

flat-sided container to her lips. She was still more gone than awake, but even so she tried to resist the liquid.

"It's all right, ma'am. I brought this water with me. It's all right."

He could not tell if she was awake enough to understand him or if the pressing greed of thirst overcame her reluctance. Whatever the reason, this time she drank when he held the canteen for her. She drank in great, gulping swallows, making tiny mewling sounds low in her throat as she sucked strongly at the metal rim of the canteen.

"Good. That's good," Longarm soothed as he would have crooned to an ailing child.

The woman sighed and settled back against the pallet. He got the impression, though, that this time she was sleeping instead of unconscious. Her face relaxed, and she seemed to be resting now.

Longarm had been kneeling on the ground beside the pallet. Now he left her side and pulled one of the crates close to where she lay, upended it, and sat down. He reached for a cheroot and stared down at the sleeping woman.

He shook his head. Now that he had time to look at her, he could see that she should have been a fairly attractive female of the species.

She was young. Her complexion was good, her bone structure sound. Her hair, gathered at the nape of her neck in a thick rope of dark brown braid, was tidy.

She really should have been a presentable if rather ordinary female person.

But something—illness? near-starvation?—had made her a barely breathing skeleton. There was almost no flesh left to her. Her skin pulled tight and pale across bones so close to the surface that they looked like they were threatening to break through at any unguarded motion.

She looked as close to death as any living person Long-arm could remember seeing.

She seemed to be resting comfortably enough now, so he stood and began to make a rapid inspection of the contents of the dugout. There was little enough to find.

The few old crates held a few, very few, articles of clothing, all of which were clean, half of which were a man's. There were two tin plates, two cups, two forks, three spoons, and a single kitchen knife. There was one skillet, the pan he had used to fetch the water in, and a large pot. A cloth sack held some dried grasses and other dried and withered vegetation that might have been herbs or might as easily have been just weeds. Discoloration on the material of the cloth showed that the bag had been used to concoct a tea or beverage of some sort, although the dried stuff now in it had never been boiled.

There was no sign anywhere in the place of any kind of food. Longarm went back outside to the mare and got his saddlebags.

He cursed himself some as he came back inside, railing at his failure to pack more than a day's ration for what he had intended as a short ride out to the Three Bar Seven and a quick return to Peyton.

He had a little jerky—he always carried some of that dry staple of plains travel—and a handful of biscuits he had brought along from the leftovers at breakfast. While the woman slept, he used the handle of the kitchen knife to crush and pulverize the jerky into a lumpy powder, which he mixed with water from his canteen.

There was no wood for a fire, but bundles of dried grass had been stacked beside the fireplace. He lighted one of those with a match from his pockets—there were no matches or even flint and steel that he could find in the place—and set the pot of beef gruel on the crude grate that had been built into the rock walls of the fireplace. He shook his head a little. He was used to seeing poverty, but not to this extent. He had seen bands of Digger Indians set up better than this poor woman.

When the jerky had softened and separated into a broth of sorts, Longarm carried it to the sleeping woman.

This time he did not have to try to wake her. When he brought the pot near and hunkered at her side, her nose wrinkled and twitched in response to the strong beefy odor. A moment later her eyes opened. She did not look at her benefactor, her eyes going unerringly toward the pot he held. And she sucked with desperate hunger at the spoonfuls of broth he slowly fed her.

Chapter 13

"Blake," she said. "Ida Blake." Her voice was weak, but at least now there was a faint blush of color in her sunken cheeks. "The widow Blake, if you prefer." She said that with sadness.

Grief is a private thing. Longarm made a few noises that could be taken for sympathy and leaned forward to plump the wad of clothing he had placed behind her head. There were no pillows in the dugout, so he had had to make do.

"Is there stock that needs tending, Miz Blake?" He had already been outside to unsaddle his mare and put her in the corral, after first carefully turning off the windmill and draining the tainted water tank so she would not be affected by whatever it was that had brought Ida Blake so low. Thoughts of going on to the Three Bar Seven this afternoon had necessarily had to be put aside.

The thin woman shook her head, and again there was

sadness in her eyes. "Dead. All of them," she said. "I don't know from what. They all died."

Longarm could guess at what had killed them, but he said nothing for the moment. This hardly seemed the time for it.

While he had been outside he had taken a look at the well casing beneath the windmill tower. The packing looked as if it had been removed and only partially replaced. It would have been no great trick for some murderous son of a bitch to drop a package of rat killer or some other toxic substance down into the well. There was no telling how long such a substance would continue to feed into the water supply for human and animal here.

"Are you really a deputy marshal?" she asked.

"Yes, ma'am." He had already shown her his badge, but he guessed that she was only marginally aware. She had been, possibly still was, very close to death herself.

"You aren't one of those murderers?" she asked.

"No, ma'am," he said patiently.

She sighed and seemed content for the moment. She allowed her eyes to sag shut, but soon opened them again. "They said it was an accident, you know."

"What was that, ma'am?"

It took her another moment to focus on the conversation. "When Murray died. They said it was an accident. I know that it wasn't."

"Really?"

She nodded. "A month ago, it was. They said his horse fell with him. But he had marks on both sides of his head. I knew it wasn't an accident. But they buried him before that young deputy could get out from town to see him. But I knew, you see. I told them so. I was going to go to town and make a complaint. And I will too. But I've been sick."

She sighed. "So sick. I don't understand that. I'm not the kind for getting sick. I never do. But this time..." Her voice faded away and for a few seconds it was as if she slept. Then her eyes popped open and she resumed the conversation as though it had never been interrupted, or as if she did not know that it had. "I still intend to make a complaint, you understand. Could you help me do that?"

"If you wish, ma'am." He thought it best not to go into any complicating details about jurisdictions. Better to ease her mind and mention it to Race Glesson when he got back to Peyton.

Mrs. Blake smiled. She closed her eyes and wriggled closer into the pallet. This time she slept deeply.

Longarm did not want to leave her alone in this condition, but he had little choice. The few scraps of jerky he had brought with him were not enough to give her the nourishment she needed. More important, his two-quart canteen could not begin to fill the needs of two people and a horse. He had to find both food and water if he intended to nurse Mrs. Blake back to health, or to some approximation close enough so that he could get her moved into town, where she could be properly taken care of. Even if the little mare would pull in harness, there was no wagon or buggy in the yard he could use to move her, and she certainly would not be in any condition to ride for quite some time.

He emptied his canteen into the cooking pot and went back out to saddle the mare again.

Finding food was not a problem here. His Winchester and the first antelope he saw took care of that. Within little more than minutes he had a haunch of fresh meat tied behind his cantle.

Finding water turned out to be much more difficult. There seemed to be no shortage of water underground, as the windmills he had already seen in this country so aptly showed, but surface water was something else entirely. At this season the washes and creekbeds were dry, and if there were ponds or lakes in the area he did not know how to find them.

Eventually, late in the afternoon, he spotted the vanes of a windmill to the north and rode toward them.

The windmill dominated a shallow basin that was filled with pens and chutes and weatherbeaten buildings. A sprawling house, added to many times, was on the east side of the complex, a collection of sheds and a bunkhouse on the west. In between were more sheds and a haphazard run of corrals and sorting pens. Horses, light saddlers and heavy cobs, milled in the corrals. Several people were visible, moving from one building to another. Longarm rode down to them.

The nearest man was tall and gray-haired, with a drooping moustache and a suspicious look in his eyes. "You don't look like a grubline rider." He grunted. "But the cookshack's over there. We don't feed till all the hands are in. You can wait if you're of a mind to."

"Is this the Three Bar Seven?" Longarm guessed.

"What of it?"

Longarm introduced himself. "I need to talk with one of your men," he said, "but I'll have to come back and do that tomorrow. Right now I need to borrow a water bag from you, if you have one, and water from your well. Some bread or biscuits too, if your cook could spare some."

"Why?"

Longarm told him. The man grunted again, without apparent friendliness or concern. "Damn fool woman. I told her she shoulda left after her man got killed."

"I don't think this is exactly the time to go into that," Longarm reminded him. "Right now I'm more interested in

99

keeping her alive than worrying about her wisdom or lack of it. Can I borrow the stuff or not?"

The man seemed to think about it for a moment before he finally grunted and nodded a grudging assent. He turned and barked out a name and one of the nearby hands came over. "Toby will get you what you need," he told Longarm. He turned and walked, stiff-backed and erect, toward the main house.

Toby brought Longarm a canvas water bag and a gunny sack containing a loaf of freshly baked bread and several cans of peaches. He handed them up to the federal man and walked away without bothering to say goodbye.

Friendly crowd, Longarm thought as he reined the mare away. Never once had they expressed concern for Mrs. Blake's welfare, or had anyone invited Longarm to dismount. He had also noticed that everyone he had seen on the place was middle-aged or older.

Still, they had given him what he had asked for. Nothing more than that, but they had done that much, at least. It was something to be grateful for, he supposed.

He bumped the bay into a lope and headed back for the Blake homestead as quickly as he could.

Longarm woke to the sound of a choking moan and a soft thrashing of bedclothes. His hand had gone automatically to the butt of his Colt when he heard the first sound. Now he shoved the weapon back into its holster and left his blankets. He knelt beside the woman in the darkness. "Ma'am?"

She continued to writhe and qroan.

"Are you all right, ma'am?" He groped in the dark to find her forehead. The hair he touched was sopping wet, plastered close against her skull. Her forehead was cool to the touch and running with cold sweat. She was shivering violently, wracked with the chills that follow fever.

Longarm crawled the few feet to the pallet he had made for himself on the floor and gathered up his own blankets to add to those already piled over her. He tucked them in around her, but the extra weight seemed to do no good. He suspected that in her failing condition she did not have enough body heat left to warm herself no matter how many blankets he used to cover her.

He slipped under the blankets beside her and wrapped his arms and legs around her, adding his warmth to her as best he could, holding her against the shivering and the pain that was in her.

"It's all right. You're going to be all right now," he soothed. He stroked her head and tried to comfort her.

After a few minutes it seemed to have helped. She became quiet in his arms. She babbled something he could not understand and then, quite clearly, said, "Murray." Her arms came around him and she kissed him with a desperate need. Her breath had the sour taste of sickness, but he did not try to pull away from her. It was a small enough form of comfort he could offer.

Another minute and she became completely still in his arms. She was no longer shaking.

He was glad that the fever seemed to have subsided.

But then, with real regret, Longarm realized that the fever and all else had subsided from her for all time.

He left the pallet and reclaimed his blankets after drawing her eyes closed for the last time.

In the morning he found the place where her husband had been buried. He placed her into the ground at her husband's side and put a hastily carved wooden marker over her head. He wondered if there was anyone who would care enough to erect a proper stone for her. Probably not. Not for her or for a thousand men and women like her across the face of this hard land.

He sighed and wondered too the name or names of the people she had wanted to complain about after the death of her husband. Too late, he wished he had pressed her for an answer to that question while he had had the chance. Now he might never know.

He saddled the bay mare and gathered up the things he had borrowed from the Three Bar Seven. He did, after all, still have work to do.

Chapter 14

"You again," the gray-haired rancher said. He managed to make it sound like an accusation.

"I told you yesterday that I need to talk with one of your men. Besides, I want to return the things you loaned me." Longarm hefted the sack the hand named Toby had given him. It held the now empty water bag and an unopened can of peaches.

"My people are all out workin'. I don't pay a man to lay up in the bunkhouse."

"You're the boss, then." It was not a question—that much had been obvious—but more of an invitation for the aging fellow to introduce himself.

If the man got the hint, he ignored it. "Take that stuff you're returning to the cookhouse. The hands will be in by dark. Come back then." He pulled an old-fashioned twist of evil-looking tobacco from his pocket and gnawed off a chew while he glared up at the federal deputy. Once again, Longarm had not been invited to dismount.

There seemed little point in flying into the face of such obvious, if unaccountable, hostility. Without a warrant—more to the point, without reason to seek a warrant—Deputy Marshal Custis Long had no more right to be here than a grubline drifter. He reined the bay toward the cookhouse, as he had been instructed.

When he rode away from the Three Bar Seven he did not bother to dwell on the rancher's unwelcoming attitude. It was something Longarm had seen often enough in the past. Some people had something in their pasts that they wanted to hide. Others plain and simple did not like the law or anyone who enforced it.

He rode west, back toward the mountains and the area where the survey crew had been working when they were murdered. There would be time enough later to return to the Three Bar Seven and talk with the man who had found the bodies.

There were, he discovered, very few homesteaders in the area.

Being so close to the railroads and to towns where beef, grain, and produce could be marketed, he would have expected that the land would be fairly densely occupied here, but it was past noon before he came across another dwelling.

This place was much better set up than the Blake place had been. The house was built of milled lumber; the corrals and outbuildings were sound and in good repair. The obligatory windmill sat beside a now-dry wash, spinning silently in the breeze while a slim, steel sucker rod patiently drew water from the ground. The welcome Longarm received here was quite different from that given him back at the Three Bar Seven.

"Howdy." The man was smiling before he had time to see who the visitor might be. He came out onto the front steps, pulling his suspenders over a shoulder, a mug of steaming coffee in his hand. "Light an' come in, neighbor. You've just missed dinner, but we've plenty left over. The trough's over there if you want to water the horse."

Longarm thanked him and stepped out of the saddle. He led the mare to the trough, but she was not thirsty.

"Turn her in that pen there an' let her roll while you eat," the man offered. The homesteader was short and wiry. His clothing was ragged, but his place was neat and well tended, and the animals Longarm could see in his corrals were fat. Longarm thanked him, pulled his saddle, and let the little mare lose in the pen for a midday rest.

The man had followed him out to the gate. When the mare was comfortable and a forkful of hay had been given to her he extended a hand. "Ty Whitacker," he said. "You can call me Curly." With a friendly grin, he took his hat off and rubbed a palm over a bald scalp.

Longarm laughed and introduced himself. "It's a pleasure to meet you, Curly."

"C'mon in an' eat, man."

"I'll admit that that will be a pleasure too." Longarm followed Whitacker into the small house. Most of the structure was taken up by the kitchen, which was where the family would have done most of their living. There were two people waiting inside, a young man no taller than Curly, but more stoutly built—and with hair—who was introduced as his son, Denny, and a dark-haired girl of twenty or less. "M' daughter Maggie," Whitacker said. After a moment's hesitation, he remembered to tell them who their guest was.

The family had obviously just finished their dinner. Maggie was in the process of clearing the table.

"The man's hungry, Mag," Whitacker said.

She nodded and began loading a clean plate with fried meat and boiled beans. She put a generous slab of dried-apple pie on a smaller plate for his dessert and poured coffee for all three men.

"Set, man, and get around that 'fore it gets too cold. And tell us what brings you out this way."

Between mouthfuls, Longarm told them.

Whitacker looked blank when Longarm mentioned the survey crew. "They never crossed our little place," he said. "An' I hadn't heard nothing about them being shot. But then, I don't get to town any oftener than I have to."

"I heard there was a bunch like that working somewhere around here," Denny said, "but I never seen any of them neither."

Longarm shrugged. It had been a shot in the dark anyway, a way to kill time while he waited for the Three Bar Seven people to get back to headquarters.

"There is something you might be able to help me with," Longarm said.

"Name it."

"I can't figure a motive for those boys to've been murdered," he said. "I do know they were working on a watershed survey at the time. What I wanted to know, is water a problem around here?"

"Surface or underground?"

Longarm shrugged. He really didn't know.

"Any blind man can tell you there's not hardly any standing water hereabouts," Whitacker said. "Creeks, ponds, that sort of thing, there just ain't a lot of it. But underground, hell, you can find that 'most anyplace you want to put down a well. Got to drill for it, mind. A hand-dug well, you're looking at twenty, thirty feet mostly. The water under the ground here runs mostly fifty to seventy feet. So a man's got to have a windmill. But the drilling's easy, and there's a couple different contract outfits that will do the work at a fair price. I don't reckon I've ever heard of anybody had to go down more'n ninety feet anywhere around here. You, Den?"

The younger Whitacker shook his head. "Never heard of anybody that couldn't hit water except for Sykes, an' he was sitting up on top of a mesa. Damn fool place to locate anyhow. An' the driller... it was Abe Powers that drilled for him; you remember him, Pa." The father nodded, and the son went on, "He said there was likely water on lower down, but a windmill couldn't pull it up that far, so there wasn't any point in drilling deeper. Couldn't count on an artesian flow way up there, so they quit drilling. Sykes, he hauled water up to his place in barrels for a while, but then he gave up an' moved on. Not that he came out of it so bad, though. Proved up on the homestead with cash—though where he'd have got that kind of hard money I couldn't say—and sold the place before he left."

Longarm grunted. It was a common enough story. Homesteads were easier started than kept in any part of the country. There were, of course, two ways to go about gaining legal title to homesteaded land. In either case, the land had to be claimed and improvements made. After that, though, the would-be owner could receive title from the government either by living on the land and working it for five years or, if he had money, he could live on it for just six months and then receive title by buying the land from the government at a dollar twenty-five per acre, less than that in some areas.

It was also common enough for a man who did not qualify for free homestead land to buy a short-term title by putting up the money for someone else to prove up his land and then paying the homesteader a small fee above that amount to transfer the new title. For someone who was about to lose his land and have to clear out anyway, a few dollars of profit were nearly always better than having to walk away with nothing to show for his efforts. So Longarm probably knew how this Sykes got his title money, even if the Whitackers had not figured it out.

Longarm sighed. "It sure looks like the availability of water here wouldn't have anything to do with why those boys were murdered, then."

"No way that I could think of," Curly Whitacker agreed. "Easiest thing in the world to get a well in around here."

"Well, I do thank you for the information and for the dinner," Longarm said.

"Our pleasure, Longarm. We don't see folks much. An' I wouldn't feel right if ever a man rode away from my door with his belly empty or his horse dry." Whitacker banged his empty coffee cup onto the table and stood. "C'mon, Den. We got too much work to do here for us to be layin' about all afternoon."

Denny stood and reached for his hat.

Common manners and courtesy told Longarm that his meal was finished too, even though he was not yet done with the excellent piece of pie he had been served. A stranger simply did not remain in another man's house when the owner was leaving.

"Pa?" It was the girl who had spoken. As far as Longarm could remember, that was the first word he had heard out of her.

"Yeah, Mag?"

"The marshal hasn't finished. Don't you reckon he should stay till he's done?"

"Hell, yes, Longarm," Whitacker quickly said. "Set back down there. Me and Denny have work to do, but that's no reason for you to leave now."

"If you're sure you wouldn't mind..."

"Course not." Whitacker motioned him back down into the chair. "Anything you want, you just ask Maggie. She'll fetch it for you."

"Mighty kind of you, Curly."

Whitacker waved the thanks aside and led the way out into the glare of the afternoon sunshine, Denny close on his heels. Longarm heard the sounds of trace chains jangling, and a minute later father and son drove away, Curly on a sulky mower and Denny driving a heavy wagon. This was not good country for haying, so apparently the Whitacker homestead included a bottom somewhere that would support a dry-land grain crop of some kind.

Longarm watched through the open doorway as they drove off, then turned back to his unfinished pie.

When they were well out of sight and hearing, the girl unexpectedly took a seat directly across the table from him. Until then, except for the few brief words she had spoken to her father, Longarm had scarcely been aware that she was in the room.

He looked at her now for what amounted to the first time. She was a plain girl, a trifle stocky, with drab brown hair pulled back in a severe bun. Her housedress fit her like a sack.

Longarm smiled politely. "You're a good cook, miss."

She blushed. "Thank you." She hesitated for a moment. "Ma taught me. She died last year, you know."

"No, I didn't know. I'm sorry."

The girl shrugged. She seemed to be on the brink of saying something, but holding it back. Longarm hoped it would not be the story of how she had lost her mother. Not that he was unsympathetic, but tragedies are only tragic to those who have an emotional stake in the loss.

After a moment Maggie said, "If I tell you something, Marshal, would you keep it a secret?" She sounded serious. "It's . . . why I wanted you to stay, actually."

Longarm thought that over for a minute. He did not want to deceive her. "I can promise to keep it secret, Maggie, if it isn't something that I'd have to testify to in a court of law. I won't make you any promises I can't keep. And if it's the sort of thing that I might have to talk about when I'm under oath, well, I won't pretend to you now that I wouldn't tell, because I'd have to."

"All right." Her hands fluttered a little and pulled her apron into a knot. She was looking down into her lap, not at him. "Those boys you asked Pa about?"

"Uh-huh."

"Well . . . Pa don't know this . . . an' please don't let him find out neither . . . but I knowed them. Lordy, I like to dropped the coffee pot when you said they was dead. All of them?"

He nodded.

"Would you mind telling me about it?"

He did, without going into detail.

Maggie sighed. "No wonder, then."

"No wonder what?"

She sighed again. "No wonder Pete didn't meet me like he said he'd do."

"Pete. That would have been Peter Donnelson?" It was one of the names of the dead boys that had been in the report.

Maggie nodded.

"How did you know him?" Longarm asked.

110

"He . . . well, he stopped here one afternoon. Lookin' for water an' kind of scouting out ahead of the wagon. Pa an' Denny was out working, like they are right now, an' I was here alone except for him. Like I am now, except for you. And Pete, he was an awful nice-lookin' fella." She gave him a coy little smile and added, "Like you are."

She stopped. After a moment she went on. "We got . . . acquainted. Talked some. A . . . a body gets lonesome. You know?"

Longarm nodded. "Did Pete say anything . . ."

"No," she said before he could finish. "Nothing 'bout anything that could help you. No kind of trouble or worries or nothing. I just . . . wanted to know. I mean, I was kinda sweet on him. An' I thought he was kinda sweet on me too. Not to marry or nothing like that. I'm not trying to tell you a story that wasn't so. I mean, he was a fancy feller from back East, and I know I wasn't anything to him but an ol' country girl he met for the summer. I'm not trying to say anything more than that. I mean . . . get anything out of his family or nothing. I want you should understand that, Marshal. I just . . . was feeling kinda bad when he said he'd show up an' then he didn't."

"Did he come here more than once?"

Maggie nodded. "Twicet, it was. He said he'd be back again, but he never. An' I was thinkin' maybe he found somebody he liked better. Or something." He could see the vulnerability showing on her plain, round face.

"No, Maggie, it was nothing like that. I'm sure he would have come back."

She sighed and stood and walked around behind him. Longarm assumed she was going to get the coffee pot, but she stopped behind him, and he could feel the light touch of her hand at the back of his neck.

"A girl . . . gets lonely. You know?" Her fingers gently massaged the nape of his neck. It felt surprisingly good. "No one out here but Pa and Denny. Never get to town, hardly." She leaned forward, pressing against him. He could feel the warmth of her belly against the back of his head. "You know?"

The material of the ugly housedress all of a sudden seemed very thin and flimsy. And he became aware that she smelled faintly of soap.

"You know?" she repeated.

"Yes." Longarm stood and turned.

Chapter 15

Given a choice, Longarm would much rather have been back in Peyton with Emmaline Logan. But he was not in Peyton, and Emmaline Logan was nowhere near. And Maggie Whitacker had been abundantly clear on the subject of loneliness. Besides which, he suspected it would quite genuinely hurt her feelings now if he walked out and went on about his business.

She came into his arms and held him much tighter and closer than was necessary, and he got the impression that she honestly *was* lonely, that it was not so much a wanton desire for sex that drove her into this vulnerable condition. She plain and simple wanted to be *with* someone, wanted to touch and be touched, to hold and be held; that she wanted, for however long or short a time, to have some physical and emotional contact with another human being.

He kissed her, and he could feel more than hear her sobbing as she clung to him.

"Are you all right?"

Maggie nodded. She laid her head against his chest and nuzzled him with her cheek and chin.

"You're sure?"

"Yes. Now." She sighed. This time the faint sound seemed happy.

He opened his mouth to speak, then thought better of it and remained quiet. He had been about to tell her that she did not need to buy his touch with the currency of her body, that he would gladly sit and hold her if she wished. But he was afraid that she would take it as a refusal and be hurt or that she would feel shamed for him to understand her real need. Better, he thought, to allow her to set the pace that gave her comfort. He kissed her again.

She was not pretty, rather far from it in fact, but at such close range that was not noticeable. She kissed him back with a fierce intensity, her eyes tightly shut and her body trembling.

Her hips moved and shifted against his pelvis, and he felt himself respond. She obviously felt the response too. She slid a hand between them and stroked him through the rough cloth of his trousers.

So maybe, he decided, her motives weren't *all* just a matter of being held. She certainly was not a virgin. Apparently she had awakened to the needs of the flesh as well as those of the spirit.

She was not dense, either. His momentary pause before reaction to her touch was apparently interpreted not as the moment of thought that it had been but as a possible concern.

"Pa won't be home till dark," she whispered. "He never comes in till then."

"Good," he whispered back. He hoped he sounded like he meant it.

Maggie pulled away from him with a swift, light kiss and stepped back. She untied her apron and took it off, then began to unbutton the front of her dress.

It was an offering, a gift, and he waited, watching quietly and allowing her to make the offer, extend the gift.

She shrugged the ugly housedress off her shoulders and let it fall to the floor. She wore nothing under the garment except for a pair of heavy, much-worn brogans that she kicked off. She stood naked in front of him. She looked suddenly shy.

Longarm took a moment to admire her body deliberately and slowly. He smiled at her and received a shy, slow smile in return.

In truth the gift she gave him was imperfect. She was long-waisted, her legs short and her thighs thick. Her torso was thick also, and she had a soft roll of plump belly over the curly brown patch of pubic hair. Her breasts were small and sagging, neither firm nor in proportion with the rest of her body.

But that imperfect body was all she had, and she was offering it to him.

He smiled again and pulled her to him and wrapped his arms around her. He wondered if it would be gilding the lily too much if he complimented her figure, then realized that no woman ever finds a compliment out of place. "You're lovely," he said.

Maggie sighed and wriggled happily in his arms. "I want you so much," she whispered. "I wanted you right from the minute you walked through that door. Wished Pa would go sooner." She began fumbling with his belt buckle. "You're an awful pretty man, Marshal."

115

Longarm chuckled and helped her. He pulled off his gunbelt, but continued to hold it in his hand. "Where?" he asked.

"There." She inclined her head toward one of the two doors leading to the back of the house.

Longarm slipped an arm around her somewhat thick waist and led her into the tiny room. There was a single cot in it and a small bureau and nightstand with a candle instead of a lamp. He placed the gunbelt on the nightstand and let Maggie go back to the business of his buttons.

She helped him off with his boots and out of his clothes. When he was undressed she giggled with pleased surprise and played with him, running her fingertips up and down the length of him.

"So big," she marveled.

"You aren't disappointed?"

She laughed happily and hugged him.

"Good," he said.

They lay on the small cot, Maggie wedged between Longarm's lean frame and the hard wall, and he took his time about kissing her, tasting her mouth, tonguing her lips and teeth and eyelids. Maggie wriggled and squirmed with joy. All the while she held onto him with her arms and one plump leg.

He fondled her breasts. They were so soft, and her skin tone so weak, that they ran in his fingers like warm whipped cream, but her nipples, small and dark, were as hard as acorns.

He rolled her nipples between the pads of his fingers and Maggie moaned. Her head lolled back onto the grass-stuffed sack that was her pillow, and her lips parted and pulled away from her teeth in an involuntary grin of pleasure. She groaned.

She was warm and she was willing, but she was neither worldly nor greatly experienced, certainly not to the extent of being an imaginative or inventive bedmate. He would gladly have shown her new paths to pleasure, but before he had time for any of that she was pulling and twisting and trying to position him.

"Now," she said.

"So soon?"

"Now."

He raised himself partway off the narrow cot and let her slide underneath him. She opened herself to his entry and reached between them to guide him into her wet, waiting body.

Maggie's legs came up and clamped around his waist, and she wrapped her arms all the tighter around him as he eased gently inside her.

She bit at her lower lip and her eyes lost their focus as he socketed full depth into her body. She mumbled something into his ear that he did not understand and began to pump her hips up and down in time to some unheard rhythm of the flesh.

Longarm let her set the pace, stroking with her, shallowly at first, gradually taking and giving longer and stronger strokes as the speed of her movements built and her breathing quickened.

He could feel her build beneath him, the intensity of her lovemaking rising, until after scant minutes she cried out and clutched at him convulsively with arms and legs and greedy mouth.

She stiffened and arched her hips high, straining to receive the last scrap of hot male flesh into herself, and Longarm pounded her stomach with his belly in a last driving frenzy of motion.

When she went limp and collapsed under him in an abrupt relaxation that was almost like a faint, she pulled away from him and he sprang free of her moist grasp.

He lowered himself gently on top of her—the cot was not big enough for him to lie beside her—and he could feel his still quite stiff erection throbbing between his belly and hers.

"You're still so *big*," she whispered.

"I haven't made it yet," he said with a smile.

"But..."

"There's time. We aren't in any hurry at all. We have lots and lots of time, dear Maggie. And, personally, I want to enjoy every minute of it."

Maggie smiled and ran her hands up and down the hard, muscled planes of his back.

"I'm *so* glad you came by today, Marshal."

"So am I," he assured her. He kissed her. A thought came to him, and he had to struggle to keep from smiling in the middle of the kiss. The only thing that he could remember her calling him was "Marshal." He wondered if...no, by golly, at this point he suspected that the darn girl hadn't caught his name when her father made the introductions.

He threw his head back and laughed.

"What is it?"

He shook his head, still chuckling. He hugged her and felt the warmth of her arms as she hugged him back. "Nothing, Maggie. Just happy, is all. Having a good time."

Maggie laughed and kissed him joyously. "So am I, Marshal. So am I."

Chapter 16

It was past eleven o'clock before Longarm finally rode the tired little mare into Peyton and gave her a well-earned rubdown and graining in the shed behind Mrs. Rurick's house.

Longarm was nearly as tired as the mare—it had been that kind of wearisome day—but there was a light burning inside the Glesson home. He ignored the lure of soft bed and deep sleep and walked the short distance to Race Glesson's parents' house.

Race's mother answered the door. Longarm removed his Stetson.

"Yes, Marshal?" She did not sound or look particularly pleased to see him.

Longarm apologized for the interruption. "I was wondering if Race might still be awake, ma'am."

Mrs. Glesson did not receive that with any particular

favor either. She frowned, but she let Longarm into the small vestibule. "I think he is. I took him some milk and cookies just a little while ago. Wait here while I see if he is asleep yet."

Longarm managed to suppress the smile that wanted to come to his lips. Race Glesson was probably in his twenties and was grown man enough to hunt other men for the law, yet his mother still brought him milk and cookies. Actually, Longarm reflected, that was a rather nice commentary on the Glesson family in particular and on mothers in general, bless them. He waited while Mrs. Glesson disappeared inside her home. A minute later she came back. Reluctantly she said, "He is still awake."

She led Longarm back to the bedroom, where Race was propped up against a thick stack of feather pillows.

The young county deputy smiled a welcome.

"How are you feeling?" Longarm asked.

"Fine. Will be, anyhow. No sign of poison in the wound, so it'll come along, given enough time. The question is, how are *you* doing?"

"I'm not the one that was shot."

"No, but you're the one that's still working," Race said. "Have you learned anything?"

"Mighty little," Longarm admitted. "I finally got to talk with Alvin Kestle this evening. Found him out at the Three Bar Seven at supper time. The boss out there wasn't willing to call Kestle in during the day. Man, that's an unfriendly bunch."

Glesson shrugged. "Notional, for sure. Old man Walker has been here practically forever, at least compared with the rest of us. He came up to this country 'way back, out of Texas during the War, I think it was. That might not sound long to you, but around here it makes him a genuine oldtimer."

"Out of Texas during the War, huh?" Longarm did not comment further, and Race Glesson was probably too young to understand the implications of that simple statement, but to anyone old enough to remember, it made one wonder what kind of man this Walker was.

Even the fiercest die-hards of the G.A.R., the staunchest of staunch Union supporters, had come to respect the Rebs who poured out of Texas by the thousands back in those now-distant days. Whether a man believed them to have been right or totally wrong, they had earned both fear and respect for their fanatic devotion to their failed cause. Texas had virtually stripped itself of its menfolk in support of the Confederacy. And the very few who had not gone off to fight for the South had marched off with every bit as much raw determination to fight for the North. In Texas there had been no middle ground.

But Walker had pulled out and come here to Colorado, then a gold-greedy territorial possession of the United States with a ready market for all the beef he could produce.

Apparently this Mr. Walker was a man who chose to look out for his own interests first.

Which was, of course, very much the same impression the man had given in the flesh.

"Did you learn anything from Kestle?" Race asked.

"Nothing I hadn't already heard from you."

Glesson reached for a glass that still had some milk in it. He had difficulty reaching it on the small table that had been placed beside his bed, and Longarm fetched it for him.

"Thanks." He swallowed down the milk and made a face.

Longarm laughed.

Glesson made another face and said, "Easy enough for you, but you oughta try being nursed by my mom." He grinned. "I don't think I'm ever gonna be able to enjoy chicken soup again in my life."

"Next time I come I'll slip a half-pint into my pocket for you."

"Would you?" Race sounded genuinely eager about the prospect.

"It's a promise."

"You just might save my life if you'd do that, Longarm." He grinned again.

"Then I'll do it for sure."

"Nobody shot at you this time out, huh?"

Longarm shook his head. "But I haven't forgotten about the bastard. And I'm not exactly riding so as to make it easy for him, neither. Whoever he is, I want him just about as bad as you do."

Race nodded.

"What I dropped by to tell you tonight was about a woman dying in your jurisdiction, Race. A Mrs. Blake. Widow woman."

Race looked truly upset by the news. "Damn," he muttered.

"You knew them?"

"Murray and Ida Blake. Sure I knew them. Awful good folks, the kind any piece of country always needs more of. What happened that Ida's dead?"

Longarm told him. Glesson's response was an angry struggle to push himself upright. Longarm thought he was going to come out of the bed and hurt himself. He had to physically push the young deputy back against the pillows to make him hold still.

"Calm down, Race. You can't do anything about it until you heal."

"But damn it, man, those were good people. And, by God, they were *my* people. This is my end of the county and I'm not gonna have some sorry son of a bitch poisoning wells and harming people around here."

"I know, Race. That's why I wanted to tell you about it right away. But first you have to get well enough to walk and ride. Right now you can't do but so much to help." He paused. "This isn't a federal matter, of course, so I don't actually have jurisdiction. But I don't think there's anything in the rules that prohibits me from helping the local law any way I can. I want you to know, if there's anything I can do, I'll damn sure do it."

Race leaned back against the pillows, a look of helpless frustration on his young features.

"Can you think of anybody who might want to harm the Blakes?" Longarm asked.

Without hesitation, Glesson shook his head. That was an immediate and personal response, though. He apparently realized that, because he hesitated and gave the question some thought before he actually answered.

"You didn't know those folks, of course, Longarm, but when they made up the phrase 'salt of the earth' they were talking about the Blakes an' folks like them. Real good people. Murray came out here last year. From Indiana, I think it was. That old saying about not having a pot to piss in? That was Murray. Couldn't afford train fare so he drove out in the farm wagon. Didn't even have a canvas cover for it. They slept under the wagon. Ida was his second wife. His first died trying to have their first child, an' the child died too. I guess Murray was ten years or so older than Ida.

"Anyway, he came out here with just damn near nothing. He'd been tenant farming back East and had this dream about being his own man, making his own place in the world. So they up and came out here and filed on that homestead. He had to trade labor to get his well drilled and

123

beggared himself to buy the mill and hardware. Swapped more labor to get lumber to build the tower. I mean, he was a worker. He had more gumption than just about anybody I've ever known. And he was gonna make it. I believe that, Longarm. Murray was gonna make it on that dry-land homestead. He was flat gonna build a future for him and Ida on that little piece of ground." Race shook his head sadly.

"Do you know what happened to him?"

Race shrugged. "Accident. It was . . . oh . . . three, four weeks ago. A horse fell with him. He was trading labor again. Swapping a week's work for a fresh cow and her calf. Something like that."

"Who was he riding for at the time?" Longarm asked.

"Three Bar Seven," Race said. "They're pretty much neighbors, you know. Not that Walker is much of a neighbor, but he's a penny-pinching old son of a bitch and I guess he figured it was cheaper to cull out a poor cow than hire another rider for cash money."

"Uh-huh." Longarm fingered his chin and reached for a cheroot. "Mind if I smoke?"

Glesson looked toward the doorway. The door was shut. "Got two of them?"

Longarm smiled and nodded. He gave one to Race and struck a match to light both cigars. Glesson took a deep pull on the cheroot, coughed once, then relaxed. "Ahhh. Nice."

"Good." Longarm examined the end of the cheroot. The coal was burning evenly. "How'd you hear about Blake's accident?"

"As a matter of fact, it was Kestle who brought the word to me. Just a coincidence, though, I'm sure. He said they were all there at the branding when Murray's horse went down. Said the whole crew saw it, but there wasn't anything anybody could do to help. By the time they got to him it was too late for that. You know how it is."

Longarm nodded. "I've known a lot of good boys who've gone under that way. No need to investigate an accident like that."

"No," Race agreed. "Sure was a pity, though." He sighed. "I surely did intend to get out and speak with Ida afterward. See if there was anything I could do to help. You know." He sighed again. "Somehow I just never made it out there."

"You couldn't have known there was any need to be in a hurry about it."

"No, but that's a poor enough excuse, isn't it?"

"Blake was helping them brand, huh?"

"That's what Kestle said."

"Kind of early for branding. A man usually waits for cooler weather before he starts bothering his cattle with branding."

"True, but the Three Bar Seven started early this year. Walker's been talking about selling out an' retiring somewhere. I hear he wants to have a complete head tally so he won't have to sell by book count, an' he wants to have all the work done and ready for a buyer to come in and take over as quick as the cash is paid."

"Pretty big outfit, the Three Bar Seven," Longarm observed.

"Not so big by some standards, I guess, but it's the biggest around here."

"Deeded land?"

"Some. Some deeded and some leased, and I guess the most of it open range grazing."

"Open range gets smaller all the time," Longarm said.

"That's likely one of the reasons Walker wants to sell. He's used to doing things the old ways. Of course he has plenty under lease, and a lease transfers the same as deeded ground when you sell a place. Even if he didn't have a single acre of open range available, he'd have plenty enough to attract a buyer."

"You don't know if he's found anybody to buy, do you?"

Race shrugged. "Rumor has it that there's a syndicate back East that's interested, but nobody's showed up to look at the place yet. I'd have heard for sure if anybody actually came out and inspected it."

"Rumors aren't always right, either."

"That's for sure," Race said. He took another pull on the cheroot and examined the tip admiringly. "I sure am glad you stopped in here tonight, Longarm. In spite of the bad news."

"The news wouldn't have been any different if you'd heard it some other time. And for more reasons than you might suspect, I'm glad I stopped in tonight too."

They chatted for a few minutes more, and Longarm left. Mrs. Glesson seemed glad to see him go. She undoubtedly was thinking that Race needed rest more than he needed to be bothered by some dang federal man tonight. Probably, Longarm admitted, she was right.

He walked back to the boardinghouse and let himself quietly in through the back door so he would not disturb anyone else's rest.

Chapter 17

The door to Longarm's room was slightly ajar. He had not left it that way.

Longarm paused in front of the unlocked and partially open door. Certainly there were any number of logical and perfectly legitimate reasons why it might be that way. Before he left he had made sure Mrs. Rurick knew he would be returning, but that he might be gone as much as several days before he did come back. She might well have decided to clean the room for him while he was away and left the door that way when she was finished.

Or Linny Logan could have come back for a repeat performance. She could have come back this evening or even last night and failed to close the door completely when she slipped out again. Certainly she would not want anyone to hear her leave. She would have excellent reason to be wary of the sounds of doors being closed.

Sure, Longarm thought. The damn thing could also have been left open by Santa Claus making pre-season checks of all the households in Peyton.

The fact was, he did not *know* what had happened. And he was not going to take any chances. The double-action Colt filled his hand, and he slipped silently down the hallway to blow out the night lamp hanging on the wall.

The probability that anyone was still inside that room waiting for him was very small. But until he knew for certain that he was alone in the darkened room, he was not willing to stand in a lighted hallway while he opened that door. He blew the lamp out and soft-footed back the way he had come, feeling along the wall for the correct door opening.

He was still two paces away from the door when he heard a muffled thump. He froze in place, senses straining to hear, even to smell whatever or whoever was in there.

There was another thump and quickly the sounds of grunting.

Someone was engaged in a struggle inside that room.

That meant there had to be at least *two* people in there.

He heard the sound of something falling to the floor. From the dull, heavy quality of the thump he thought it might have been a human body.

He stepped forward, found the door opening with his left hand, and began to ease into the totally dark room.

Something—some*one*—bumped into his right shoulder. It startled the intruder. Longarm heard a gasp of surprise.

Whoever it was, though, had excellent reflexes. A fist or an object—whatever it was, it was extremely hard—smashed into Longarm's stomach just as his own reactions sent the butt of the heavy Colt slashing at head height in front of him.

The Colt connected with something. A head, he thought.

There was an outrush of air. Pain this time, not surprise. And something struck his right arm with vicious force.

The revolver spun out of Longarm's numbed fingers and fell loudly to the floor.

Longarm instinctively lashed out with his left fist, low and hard and sweeping forward. He felt the fist go deep into a man's belly, and there was the sound of a cough or withheld outcry.

He struck again with his right. He could not be sure of making a fist with the numb fingers and did not want to risk breaking his hand, so he smashed out and down with his clubbed forearm and felt it strike hard flesh.

The intruder caught him in the kneecap with a kick. Longarm's leg was twisted aside and he lost his balance for a moment.

The moment was enough. The intruder bulled forward, knocking Longarm aside.

Longarm fell sprawling onto the floor. He rolled aside immediately, but he did not have to worry about anyone shooting. Not now.

He heard the unseen intruder race through the door and down the hall, boot heels loud on the planks.

Longarm picked himself up and rubbed his right arm. The feeling was starting to return now. The arm was not broken.

He lit a match, intending to find the Colt he had dropped.

The light revealed the motionless body of Linny Logan on the floor beside the bed. She was naked.

Beyond the door, in the hallway, Longarm could hear more footsteps. It was a lighter, quicker tread than the intruder's had been.

"Mr. Long? Mr. Long, is that you?"

It was Mrs. Rurick's querulous voice.

"Yes, ma'am." Longarm quickly blew out the match he still held and hurried to the door. He held it nearly closed and spoke to her from behind it. "Sorry, ma'am. The hall lamp wasn't on, and I stumbled trying to find my room. I'm sorry if I woke you."

For a moment there was no answer, then the sound of a short sniff of displeasure. "Very well, Mr. Long."

"Good night, ma'am."

The only response was the sound of her footsteps fading into another part of the house.

Longarm felt a moment of relief. But only a moment. If Linny Logan was dead . . . He shook his head. Time enough to worry about that if it was so.

He groped first on the floor for his Colt and returned it to the cross-draw holster over his left hip, then felt his way to the window to make sure the curtain was drawn and the blind down. He was not about to light a lamp inside the room if there was a chance that the would-be assassin was still outside watching the place.

Only when he was sure the recent intruder could not see did he hunt for the lamp and strike another match.

Linny Logan was still on the floor, but she was moving now, making feeble, brushing motions with her hands as if she was trying to frighten away flies from her stomach.

Longarm knelt beside her. "Linny? Emmaline?" He smoothed her hair and shook her lightly by the shoulders. Damn, but she was a good-looking woman. Even in his concern for her safety he could not help but respond to the sensuality of her unclothed body.

He leaned close and whispered her name into her ear. He did not dare speak aloud, for fear that Mrs. Rurick would still be prowling in the hall.

After a moment she opened her eyes. It took her a second

or two to focus. Then her eyes widened. "Custis. What happened?" She began to cry, and he cradled her in his arms and tried to soothe her.

"I was hoping *you* could tell *me* what happened," he said when she seemed calmer.

"I don't know. I . . . I came in a little while ago. I saw you ride into town, so I knew you'd be coming here. I wanted to surprise you, be here when you arrived."

"You did surprise me," he said.

"It was dark. I didn't want to light the lamp, of course. I wanted to surprise you, after all. And I thought Mrs. Rurick might knock if she saw a light under the door. So I took my things off and got into bed to wait for you. And then . . . I don't know . . . a few minutes ago, I guess, the door opened. I thought it was you. I couldn't see. He slipped in so fast I couldn't see except to know it was a man. I thought it was you." She sounded frightened, and Longarm stroked the back of her head and petted her.

"He left the door open just a bit," she went on. "Not much, but a little. I could see, just a little, enough to see where he was. It was very dark."

"Sure," Longarm assured her.

"He came over to the bed and sat down. I guess he was going to wait for you, but I was still thinking it was you and that you were going to take your boots off or something. You have to understand that I really did think it was you, Custis. I mean, I don't *do* that sort of thing with just *any-body.*"

"What sort of thing, Linny?"

"I . . . Well, I put my hand in his crotch. You know. It was *you* I wanted to surprise, Custis." She shuddered. "I surprised him, all right."

If it hadn't been so damned serious, it would have been

funny. Longarm could well imagine the shock the bastard must have gotten.

Sneak into an empty room like that, waiting there to murder a man, and all of a sudden something gropes your balls. Yeah, Longarm could well imagine that the guy was surprised. Probably crapped in his drawers.

"He . . . hit me, Custis. I knew already that it wasn't you, of course, but I certainly didn't expect him to hit me." She shuddered again. "It was awful."

"You said you already knew it wasn't me?"

She nodded.

"How?"

"When I reached around to touch him . . . touch you, I mean . . . I didn't grab his thing like I thought I would. He had a flabby old roll of belly. I touched that." She made a sour face. "Ugh." She made it seem almost as if it had been worse to touch the man's fat than it had been to be hit by him. "So I knew then it wasn't you. You're all hard and flat and nice there. Not like him at all."

The killer was a fat man, then. A strong fat man. It was more than Longarm had known before. Quick son of a bitch too.

"Are you all right now, Linny?"

She thought for a moment and then nodded. "I guess so." She felt the side of her head. "He hit me here. With an elbow, I think. And I tried to get away from him. I didn't want to wrestle with him, believe me, but we got kind of tangled up in the sheet and everything, and then he hit me again and I guess I fell down to the floor here. After that everything is hazy, like I was dizzy. I could hear, but it was like I couldn't do anything about it. I just stayed there and hoped he would go away. And then he did and you lit the lamp, and I guess that's just about everything I can remember."

"You did just fine, Linny. Everything is going to be all right now." He leaned closer, just to make sure, and parted her thick blonde hair to make sure the skin had not been broken. She was not bleeding. She winced when he touched her and probably by morning she would have a goose egg there, but she seemed to be well enough after the ordeal.

Linny sighed and pulled him even closer, her arms curling around his neck and drawing him insistently toward her lips. "I feel much better now that you are here, Custis."

Longarm allowed her to kiss him. It was, after all, the polite thing to do under the frightening circumstances. The poor girl definitely needed comforting now.

Linny's ice-maiden public image was a lie of the first order.

Sweat-slick and flushed from exertions already completed, she had a level of sexual energy that would exhaust a jackrabbit.

While Longarm lay on the damp sheets of the bed and tried to recuperate with a cheroot, Linny squirmed down to the foot of the bed and lay on top of his leg. She captured his right foot between her thighs and wiggled.

"Haven't you had enough for the moment?"

"No." No equivocation whatsoever. The answer was simple and direct. She hefted his sagging member on her fingertips and gave him a feline smile. "Lovely," she declared.

"Tired," he said.

"We'll see." She gave him that smile again and rubbed her cheek along his flaccid shaft.

"Definately tired," Longarm assured her. He had come several times already, and it had been a long day before that. A man could only expect so much from himself.

Linny wriggled down farther onto his trapped foot. Her rump, shapely and pink and rounded, humped upward and then settled back down. Longarm was startled. He could feel his toes slide into the wet entrance as she captured him in quite a new way. His surprise must have shown. Linny smiled that odd smile again and moved her hips slowly, grinding him into her insatiable flesh.

While she was doing that, she drew him softly into her mouth and sucked while she humped his foot.

She was already thoroughly aroused, and she had a quick trigger anyway. After no more than a minute he could feel her body stiffen.

The pull of her pussy around his toes clutched with an increasingly insistent force, and she shuddered her way to a climax, all the while continuing to suck him deep into her mouth.

Her fingernails scraped lightly, teasingly against the underside of his scrotum, and one finger played gently around the rim of his ass.

In spite of himself, Longarm felt the stirrings of an erection. He was tired, and he almost did not *want* the damn thing.

Almost. Besides, it was already too late. Linny had felt the growth as soon as Longarm did.

She released him from her mouth and looked up at him. She smiled. She gave him a loud, moist kiss on the tiny opening from which the goodies came. She chuckled.

"Okay," he admitted. "Not *that* tired."

"We'll work on it," Linny told him.

She climbed up his frame and straddled his hips, raising herself over his now pulsing member and skewering herself expertly down onto him. He reached up and took a double handful of firm, warm tit while Linny threw her head back and arched her neck. She strained and pumped and worked very hard at it.

Longarm lay there and let the girl ride. He still had the stub of his cheroot clenched between his teeth. He laughed and let the damn girl have her way with him.

Chapter 18

It was not Longarm's custom to carry the Winchester with him when he was in town, but now he did. Whoever the damned would-be assassin was, he was determined about it, and Longarm was taking no chances now that he might be caught in the street with only a revolver for defense and a rifleman potting at him from long range.

Over breakfast at Jacob Faust's eatery, Longarm chewed on more than the pork chops and fried eggs Jacob brought him.

He still had no idea if the gunman had any connection with the deaths of the boys on the survey crew, but he tended to doubt that it did. The man had taken his first crack at the federal deputy soon after the visit to Monument. And that was simply too soon for there to be any likelihood that the shootings were connected with this investigation.

But, damn it, a stranger in Peyton would surely be easy

to spot. Longarm wished that Race Glesson was on his feet and able to help. The local man would quickly spot anyone who was out of place, though Longarm could not.

However, Longarm thought, there was always an alternate approach to any problem.

"Jacob."

"Yep?"

"When you have a few minutes, I'd like to talk to you."

"Sure."

Longarm drank coffee and waited patiently until the breakfast crowd thinned and finally disappeared. The one-armed cook cleared the emptied tables and piled the dirty dishes into a galvanized steel washtub in the back room of the restaurant. Apparently someone else came in, possibly Faust's wife, to handle that chore for him.

As soon as the immediate work was done, Jacob poured himself a cup of coffee and brought it to Longarm's table. He sat. "What's on your mind now?" he asked.

"I need some help, Jacob."

"With the killings of those boys?"

"Probably not."

Faust shrugged. "Not that it matters. I was just hoping. Like I told you before, I thought those boys were all-right kids. I'm just anxious for whoever shot them to be brought in."

"So am I, Jacob, but right now I'm concerned about something else. I'm looking for someone who doesn't belong in Peyton. At least I'm pretty sure it wouldn't be anyone local. The only thing I know about him is that he's a heavy-set man. Has a gut on him."

"That isn't a hell of a lot to go on," Faust said.

"No, but right now it's all I have."

Faust mulled that over and took a swallow of steaming

137

hot coffee. He did not seem to mind the heat. "How recent would this fellow have gotten here?" he asked.

"After I did."

Faust thought for another moment, then shook his head. "Sorry. I'd help you if I could, Longarm, but I can't think of anybody new in town who showed up after you did. Certainly none that's come in here for his meals. I could ask around, if you like."

"I'd appreciate it, Jacob." Longarm did not allow his disappointment to show. He had been hoping that in a town the size of Peyton a second stranger would have been readily located. He . . .

Longarm snapped his fingers and smiled. He leaned back in his chair, reached for his coffee cup with one hand, and pulled a cheroot from his pocket with another.

"Have yourself an idea?" Faust asked.

"An idea. Of course, it might not be worth anything, but it's sure an idea."

Faust nodded. "I hope it works out for you, then."

"We'll see."

Longarm paid for his breakfast and walked across the street to the general mercantile.

"Mornin'," the proprietor greeted him.

"Howdy."

"If you'll give me your list I'll fill it for you."

"No list," Longarm said. "Tinned meat. Half a dozen cans. Coffee, ground and bagged, not raw beans. Call it half a pound. Dried fruit. Say, three pounds. An assortment of whatever you have, but I'm real fond of the apricots." He thought for a moment. "I think that will do it."

The clerk nodded and started moving from shelf to shelf. "Box or bag?" he asked.

"A stout sack, if you have one."

"I have one." The man finished assembling the items and put them into an empty flour sack which he tied shut with twine. He licked the tip of a lead pencil and made some calculations on a notepad. "Two ten," he said.

Longarm paid him and left.

He got his saddlebags from his room and crammed the food inside them. The telegraph key and lockpicks he left behind in his valise. He doubted he would be needing those and he intended to travel light.

He found Mrs. Rurick in her kitchen and paid her in advance for a week's lodging. "If I'm not back in that time," he said, "don't worry about it. Please keep my things in the room. It might be late when I do get in."

"As you wish," she said. She eyed him with suspicion and added, "I do expect that you will be sober when you return this time, Marshal."

"Yes, ma'am, but I was sober last night too. Like I told you then, the light was out and I stumbled."

She looked skeptical, but did not say any more.

Longarm went around back of the house to the shed and saddled the bay mare. The night's rest seemed to have done her more good than it had Longarm. But then, she had been able to rest after she was put up the night before. He had remained busy for some time afterward, not all of which he regretted.

Thinking about it, he grinned at the mare, conscious of a hollow feeling low in his groin and a faint—and well worth while—soreness in that same general area.

He gave the mare a good brush-down and saddled her, taking care to smooth the blanket so she would not develop cankers over her withers. She was too good a horse to mistreat. He checked her hooves to make sure her shoes were well set and strapped the saddlebags behind the cantle.

"Ready enough," he muttered to the horse. Her ears flicked forward briefly and she snatched a last mouthful of grass hay before Longarm bridled her.

More than enough time had gone by, he thought, for anyone watching him to have set up somewhere outside of the shed, and a man in the process of mounting is at the disadvantage of momentary unbalance. He turned the mare in her stall and broached both custom and good sense—a rearing horse can smash a man's skull if there is a beam overhead—by mounting her while still inside the small building. He had to bend forward over her neck to keep from bumping his head even when she was standing quiet.

"Feel up to a little run, girl?" Bent low and forward, he put his spurs to her and the mare leaped into an almost instant run, bursting out of the shed without warning and racing out of town at a belly-down gallop. The fact that there were no shots following him meant nothing, Longarm knew. Whoever this assassin was, he was not going to be startled into a hasty shot.

Longarm drew rein and stopped to look around. He had not expected this to be easy, but *damn* there was a lot of country around here. And none of it was tall enough to give a man a good look at the rest of it. He would have appreciated a few high places from which to survey the land.

He was already sitting on top of the highest knob he could find, and all he could see around him was rolling grass, followed by more of the same.

He saw a distant flicker of motion and for a moment hoped that it might be the bastard who was stalking him. Then he realized that the motion was continuing and that it remained in one spot. Almost certainly it would be the barely visible vanes of a turning windmill.

Fair enough, he thought. He was thirsty. Probably the horse was too. And he would have to locate sources of water anyway if he intended to run this scout to a conclusion before that unknown assassin succeeded in putting a bullet under Custis Long's hide. He rode west toward the windmill, able to see it from the next rise and confirm that it was indeed a working mill over a stock tank.

The development of wind-driven pumps had sure made a difference in this country, Longarm reflected as he rode down to the tank. Over most of the country, in fact, between the Missouri and the Rocky Mountains. Now a man no longer had to depend on the infrequent streams and springs to water his stock, and as far as anyone seemed to know the water supply underground was as good as inexhaustible. He had never yet heard of a deep well going dry. The windmill, he thought, had been as important as the Homestead Act when it came to the settlement of this country.

The water in the tank was fresh and cool. A thick layer of green algae coated the sides of the steel tank. Longarm was tempted to stop long enough to take a bath in the clean water. But that would have been tempting fate and the rifleman. He dismounted, filled his canteen with fresh water, and allowed the mare to drink her fill. She was not hot, so he did not worry about her taking too much.

Whoever had built the tank, he thought, did not check it often. There was no shut-off on the pump. The mill was allowed to spin on whatever breeze there was, and the tank overflowed through a short stub of pipe, forming a tiny manmade stream with hoof-churned mud around it. The trickle of overflow water was allowed to flow south and east but disappeared far short of the dry wash Longarm could see down that way.

The hoofprints of cattle, horses, and antelope showed in

the dark red mud under the overflow pipe. The refreshing water was available to any person or animal who had need of it.

Giving the mare a rest and himself a stretch of the legs, Longarm led her away from the tank on foot. He did not feel particularly energetic, so instead of continuing west, where he would have had to climb yet another low rise, he walked southwest toward the wash. On this kind of search, one direction seemed quite as good as any other as long as all of it was eventually covered.

The thought that had come to Longarm while he was talking with Jacob Faust was simple.

The gunman was staying close enough to keep a careful eye on Longarm's movements.

Yet the man did not seem to be staying in Peyton. Unless he was a local man, which seemed unlikely, he had therefore to be camped somewhere in the vicinity of the town, somewhere fairly close to Peyton.

Close enough, perhaps, for Longarm to find the bastard's camp and lay his own ambush near it.

It certainly seemed worth a try.

And since the one time Longarm had gotten a good look at the man's line of escape, the day Race Glesson was hit by a bullet intended for Long, he had run in a northeasterly direction, Longarm was searching now in a more or less westerly and southward pattern. Most critters in flight, man included, tend to run away from their nests.

Longarm walked to the edge of the wash and looked down into it. The bottom was filled with soft sand. The ground condition was too soft to take good prints, but he could see disturbances here and there where some passing animal had been.

Very few tracks followed the course of the wash, and the sand was too fluid for him to tell what kind of animal had made those impressions.

Here and there along the sides of the wash, where the banks were low or had crumbled, he could see crossing places where livestock or game dropped down into the wash and then quickly climbed back out again. Even the wildlife seemed to know better than to stay long inside a dry wash.

Longarm looked to the south. Somewhere down there, at least according to the survey those boys had been making, any water that flowed through this wash would eventually join the Arkansas River and wind its way ultimately to the Mississippi and the Gulf of Mexico. Longarm spat into the bottom of the wash. He knew, of course, that that moisture would evaporate. But if any happened not to, why, it would someday join the salty waters of the Gulf. Hard to believe, he thought. He shrugged and mounted the steady and dependable little mare.

From the saddle he could see, a mile or more to the south, the green tops of some cottonwoods. There would be a bottom down there, he thought, probably a wide place in the long, twisting course of the wash. Someplace where the force of the occasional floodwaters that had dug the wash would be spread out enough to permit cottonwood saplings to take root and grow.

Even so, of course, it would not be wise for anyone to take shelter in that grove down there. A flood that might not dislodge a cottonwood tree could still damn well drown an unwary man if it caught him in his sleep.

He started to turn away, then stopped.

A man who did not want his camp found just might choose a place exactly like that one.

No sensible person was going to look in a damned dry wash for an enemy's camp. Not unless he thought the enemy to be a complete fool.

And what better hiding place could there be than one

that is both obvious and completely unsuspected? What better place than a grove of shady cottonwoods within the wide curve of a dry wash?

A thin smile appeared on Longarm's tanned face, and he pulled the Winchester from its boot before he eased the mare south along the rim of the wash.

Chapter 19

It was past midnight before the fat man came in to his camp. Longarm was not sure of the time. A ceiling of thin, high cloud had covered the moon some time before, and he could not read the face of his Ingersoll any longer. Not that it made any difference, but he was mighty glad he had taken the opportunity for a long nap in the afternoon after he found what he was looking for.

The camp, what there was of it, had been easy to spot despite the fat man's precautions. No gear had been left for anyone to find, and the fire ring was buried in sand and unnoticeable unless a real search was made for it. But the hole the man had dug in the sandy bottom was unmistakable, and there would have been no way the rifleman could have hidden it and still had the use of it.

The deep hole collected water for man and horse to use. Longarm had tasted of it. It was silty and thick but drinkable.

It had been the surest sign of a campsite and had convinced Longarm that this was the place where he should wait and watch, because no honest traveler was likely to go to all that trouble when a few miles of riding would take him to one of the windmills that dotted the country here.

So Longarm had picketed the bay mare several miles away, inside the hard-packed bowl of an old buffalo wallow where it would not be seen unless someone rode directly to it, and walked back to set up his vigil along the side of the dry wash.

Now the fat man was coming in. Probably, Longarm thought, he had spent the day in or near Peyton waiting for his quarry to show up. Now, disappointed and almost certainly tired, he was returning to his campsite for a few hours of sleep before the hunt would resume.

If the man's normal pattern was like this, Longarm reflected, getting into camp after midnight and having to be back on the hunt by dawn or little later, the fat man would have been living on damned little sleep for a week or better. He would not be at his peak after something like that. His thoughts and reflexes would be slowed. And besides, the hunter seldom thinks of himself as prey; a predator rarely thinks in terms of becoming the hunted. Even, Longarm had long since learned, two-legged predators.

Longarm watched while the fat man dismounted and hobbled his horse. There was little light. In the deep shadow under the cottonwood trees Longarm could see nothing, but he could make out vague shapes against the bare, sandy bottom of the wash where the man and horse now were.

The fat man unsaddled the horse and pulled its bridle. He did not brush the horse down. But then perhaps it had been used only to ride to and from Peyton.

He led it to the seep he had dug in the bottom of the

wash, where a small amount of silty water had collected during the day. He must have had a cup or pot in his hand, because he knelt and scooped something into the hole for his own water before he allowed the horse to drink. Then he let the horse drink and turned it loose to forage on the short brown grasses during the night.

The fat man went back to where he had left his saddle. He untied something from the saddle—a bedroll, no doubt— and carried the bundle into the dark shelter of the over-hanging trees.

So far, so good, Longarm thought.

The deputy lay comfortably settled on the bank of the wash opposite the grove of trees and waited. He would have enjoyed a smoke, but he was not greatly bothered by the lack. He was used to waiting.

He had decided before he ever chose his position that he would give the fat man at least an hour to fall into a deep sleep. Then he would move.

After no more than fifteen minutes he smiled to himself. An hour's wait would not be necessary. Reaching him clearly across the width of the wash, he could hear the fat man's snore.

Longarm stood and stretched. His position had not been cramped or unpleasant, but it did feel good to be able to stand and move again.

After a moment he picked up the Winchester and picked his way carefully down onto the floor of the wash. His boots made no noise in the soft sand of the bottom as he crossed the wash and entered the grove.

He moved with caution, but that was a matter of habit and prudence rather than necessity. The fat man's snoring, louder now and rasping as Longarm came closer, told him that all was well. His approach was not suspected.

Guided by the continuous nasal sawing, Longarm moved through the grove.

He reached the fat man's side and stood over him. He gave himself time for his eyes to adjust to the low level of covered moonlight here.

A rifle lay beside the fat man's blankets. Longarm picked it up and set it out of reach.

The fat man slept in his clothing, and had been doing that for some time, judging from the body odors that rose from his bed. His holstered revolver lay on ground by his head. Longarm took that too and looped the belt over his shoulder. He took two steps backward and pulled out his Colt.

Close to smiling now, Longarm reached into his pocket and found a cheroot. He bit off the end and spat it out, making no particular effort to be quiet. The rhythm of the fat man's snoring did not change.

Longarm struck a match and lighted his cigar. After the long wait the smoke tasted sharp and clean on his tongue. Still the fat man did not stir.

"Time to wake up, old son," Longarm said in a normal tone of voice.

Even then there was no change in the snoring.

"Hey!" Longarm barked loudly.

The fat man bolted into a sitting position, his hands groping first for the revolver and then for the rifle. He reached wildly around him, slapping at the ground frantically.

"Not there," Longarm told him.

The fat man looked at the tall, shadowy figure that stood over him. He blinked rapidly. He seemed to be confused, caught somewhere between sleep and fear but not fully in the grip of either. "Who . . . ?"

"Long. Deputy U. S. Marshall."

"What . . . ?"

"You're under arrest."

"But . . ."

"But me no buts, old son. I already know what you're fixing to say. You're an innocent man being put upon by the law. You're a peaceable traveler who only stopped here for a night's rest. You don't know what the hell any of this is about. You've never done a wrong thing in your life. I *know* all that. So do you. So what I advise you to do is to take down my name so when the judge acquits you, you can demand my badge. Okay? Sure. Sounds fair to me. As an innocent citizen you're bound to be let off. That's what we have courts for. In the meantime, though, old son, I strongly suggest that if you have an itch, you'd best not scratch it. Because if I see that hand of yours move another quarter of an inch I'm gonna do the prudent and sensible thing, and put a bullet between your eyes. You see, I know I have your rifle an' I have your revolver, but I don't know if you've got anything that I *don't* have. And I do not intend to take any chances. Now, do you understand me?"

The fat man was no virgin when it came to being arrested. The protests that had risen in his face were muzzled. His expression became that of the prison inmate, empty, stolid, and unquestioning.

"Fine," Longarm said. "We understand each other. Stand up, please."

The fat man did, very carefully. Without being instructed to do so, he held his hands well out to the sides of his body as he moved.

"Hands behind."

The man complied, and Longarm used his left hand to take a set of cuffs from a back pocket and clamp them around the fat man's wrists.

Even with that done, Longarm's vigilance did not relax.

He pressed the muzzle of the Colt under the fat man's ear, a reminder and a warning more than a threat, and frisked first the man's wrists and forearms.

Longarm grinned. "My, oh my, what have we here?" He pushed the man's left sleeve up, exposing a short leather gauntlet. To the gauntlet were affixed a tiny four-barreled derringer with .22 caliber bores and, in a separate pocket, a standard manacle key and a lockpick. "Nice try," Longarm said. He unbuckled the gauntlet and slipped it into his pocket. He intended to hang onto it for a while. Billy Vail would get a kick out of it.

The fat man grunted, but Longarm could not tell if the sound was supposed to be disappointment or simply an acceptance of fact.

Still nudging the man's ear with the Colt, Longarm completed his shakedown. There was another derringer of larger caliber slung in the man's crotch and a stubby, virtually barrel-less .32 rimfire revolver holstered in one armpit.

"Man, you sure must be afraid of a lightning storm," Longarm observed.

The fat man grunted again, but did not speak.

Just for the sake of insurance, Longarm frisked him again. This time he came up empty.

"You can turn around now," he told his prisoner.

The fat man did.

"Name?"

"John Smith."

"All right, Mr. Smith. Let's go find your horse and go for a moonlight ride."

Billy Vail smiled. There was neither warmth nor humor in that expression, though. At a time like this he was not the easygoing, affable fellow he normally was when he was alone with his own people.

Now the man who called himself John Smith was occupying the chair in front of the marshal's desk. Longarm and two other deputies stood nearby.

"Ask me any damn thing you want," Smith challenged again. "I gave you my name. I call it an accidental discharge of a firearm. That ain't a federal matter." He sneered. "The worst them local yahoos can give me is six months. I can do that without breaking a sweat."

Billy Vail smiled again. Longarm thought the expression looked downright nasty, actually, but Smith did not visibly react.

Nor did he say anything more, which probably was what Vail was waiting for. After several minutes Vail played another card. "Curtis Bright," he said.

Smith's eyes narrowed slightly, but he did not speak.

"The warrant says murder," Vail added. Again he waited. Again he received only silence as a response.

Billy smiled again. "Alabama has already returned an indictment," he said. "I already wired the authorities in Mobile. They are rather anxious to see you again, Curtis."

Bright blinked twice and squirmed just a little in the straight-backed chair.

"If I send you back to Alabama, Curtis, you will hang by the neck until you are dead." He smiled that tight, smug, nasty little smile again.

Bright squirmed some more.

"Don't worry, though. A man of your weight, Curtis, won't need a long fall. It won't take any time at all hardly." Vail chuckled and made a sound like a breaking twig . . . or breaking bone.

Curtis Bright paled.

Billy Vail yawned, or pretended to. He examined some papers on the top of his desk and shuffled several from one pile to another. After a minute or so he looked back up at

Bright and smiled at him. This time the smile was gentle, reassuring. "There is an alternative, Curtis."

For the first time there was a flicker of interest in Bright's eyes. But the fat man had been trained in a hard school. He did not ask the obvious question.

Billy Vail answered it anyway. "The alternative, Curtis, is that as a federal witness we would have the right to keep you here, not send you back to Alabama. We could, with an appropriate confession, prefer federal charges of assault on an officer. You could be looking at fifteen years in a federal prison instead of hanging in Alabama."

Bright coughed. He looked uncomfortable.

"The choice is yours, of course," Vail prodded. "We are entirely agreeable to whatever you want to do." He smiled the nasty smile again.

Vail waited. After little more than seconds of staring into that smile, Curtis Bright wilted. Longarm could see it in the man's face.

Bright sighed. "What do you want to know?"

"Why," Vail said. "Why were you stalking one of my people?"

"Five hundred dollars down," Bright answered, "another five hundred on delivery."

"Who?"

Bright hesitated. Longarm was not surprised. A thousand dollars was a hell of a high fee in a country where a killing could be bought for fifty. The figure implied a correspondingly high level of financial backing and need for the man who so desperately wanted him dead.

Billy Vail shrugged as if to imply that the answer meant nothing to him. The same clear choice was still present: certain death or a possible future release from jail. Vail played with the papers on his desk again.

Bright sighed. "Capperson," he said. He sounded angry. Longarm was not sure if he was angry with Capperson or with himself. It could have been either or both.

Vail smiled. "That would be Philip Y. Capperson of Capperson, Capperson and Yates?"

Bright nodded.

"I assume you will be willing to dictate a complete account of your employment and sign the statement?"

Again Bright nodded.

Billy Vail smiled. This time so did Longarm.

The information was, in a way, quite pleasing. Philip Y. Capperson was the expensive attorney representing Chester A. Watson.

"Tom, Aaron, would you please take Mr. Bright to a detention room. Find the gentleman a stenographer, please, and have his confession recorded and witnessed. Thank you."

When the room had been cleared and he was alone with Longarm again, Vail smiled. This time it was his normal mild expression. "Well, Longarm?"

"No wonder they wanted that mistrial," he observed. "They wanted time to get me out of the way. If I happened to be too dead to testify at the retrial, that rich little creep would have walked away scot free."

"As it happens," Billy said, "I would say it has worked out quite well for our side. Now we not only have Watson by the short hairs, we can nail Capperson too. Two birds with a single stone. Three, if you count Bright."

"I kinda hate to see him get off on that Alabama business," Longarm said.

Vail shrugged, but he was grinning now in a manner that Longarm found suspicious.

"Billy," Longarm said, "you're a sneaky son of a bitch

sometimes. What is it that you haven't told Mr. Bright?"

"I promised him we would not send him back to Alabama to stand trial," he said, "and of course we will not. I do not, however, make any promises regarding a murder charge in Kentucky."

"You won't mention that to him until after the Watson trial," Longarm said.

"It might slip my mind, at that," Billy admitted.

Longarm grinned at him.

"None of which," Vail said in a more serious tone, "has anything to do with the case you were theoretically investigating for the past week or so. You *have* been investigating that matter, haven't you, Longarm?"

"Yes, sir." The moment seemed appropriate for a polite response.

"Progress?"

Longarm sighed. "Nothing to brag about. But my train ride up here wasn't strictly to bring Mr. Bright in. I want to stop in at the BLM office and check some records before I go back down there."

"Line of duty, or do they have a new girl working in the office there?"

"Billy! C'mon now." Longarm tried to look innocent. Damn it, he *was* innocent this time. It *was* duty that made him want to check with that office. So why, damn it, was he finding it so difficult to *look* innocent?

Vail laughed. "Go back to work, Longarm."

The lean deputy stood and picked up his hat from the edge of the file cabinet where he had tossed it earlier. He started out.

"Longarm."

He turned. "Yes?"

"I'm reasonably glad that Bright was not successful in his mission."

Longarm grinned at him and winked. "Thanks, boss."
He left the office and headed for the Bureau of Land Management's offices.

Chapter 20

Longarm smiled. "You look better."

Race Glesson grinned a welcome. "I feel better. Why, this morning I was able to go to the backhouse by myself. Pop made me a set of crutches, so I can get around some now."

"I'm glad to hear that." Longarm liked Race. But he still felt bad about romping the girl young Race was in love with.

"You haven't been by for a couple of days," Race accused. "Have you done any good lately?"

"Some." Longarm smiled. "The fellow who owned that bullet they took out of your leg is on his way to a hanging."

The young deputy's face became animated with excitement, and he shoved himself to a more upright sitting position on the bed.

Longarm told him about it in detail.

"Then it didn't have anything to do with the shooting of

those boys down here," Race said.

Longarm shook his head. "I'm afraid not."

"Damn. I want whoever done that too, you know."

"Uh-huh."

"You don't sound too upset about it."

"I'm not," Longarm admitted.

"Something's in the wind, isn't it?"

Longarm grinned at him.

"You did find something to work on," Race went on.

He grinned again. "Could be."

"I want in on it."

"But..."

"I told you, I can get around now. I can't ride a horse,
but I can sit in a buggy seat. In this country, Longarm, I
can go anywhere you can. Whatever it is, I want to go along
with you."

"You're sure you feel up to it?"

"Hell, yes. Really."

Longarm nodded. "All right, then."

Race started to climb out of bed. His crutches were lying
on the floor beside him.

"Take it easy. It's too late to make a start this afternoon.
We can leave in the morning," Longarm told him.

"Would you leave now if you were going alone?" The
implication was clear. Glesson was not going to allow his
infirmity to slow the other lawman. If Longarm had planned
to leave—wherever it was he intended to go—this afternoon, then Race was going to leave now too, and the hell
with questions of comfort.

"Like I told you, it's too late in the day to make a start
now. We'll leave in the morning."

"Do me a favor?"

"Sure," Longarm agreed.

"Pop's wagon is a hard-sprung old son of a bitch, but

Mr. Logan has a snappy little rig that rides like a goose-down comforter. Would you ask him if I could borrow it?"

"Glad to."

Race smiled. "I've always wanted to take Linny out riding in that buggy. Damned if I don't think you make a poor substitute, Longarm."

"Damned if I don't agree with you."

They talked for a little while longer, then Longarm excused himself and left. It was getting on toward the supper hour and he wanted to catch Logan at home but did not wish to disrupt the family's evening meal.

He walked the short distance to the Logans' somewhat pretentious little house and knocked.

Linny came to the door in response. She was dressed as impeccably as the first time he had seen her. She looked lovelier than ever, pretty and sweet and virginal. Seeing her like this, Longarm could not easily envision her as the abandoned, tousled, sweaty, oversexed creature he knew her to be.

He removed his Stetson and held it politely in front of his belly. "Miss Logan."

"Marshal Long, isn't it?" She acted like a stranger, her poise completely intact.

"Yes'm."

She did not open the door to him. "What is it you wish, Marshal?"

"Is your father at home, Miss Logan?"

"We have guests at the moment, sir."

"I won't take but a minute of his time."

"Very well." She was as cold—as snooty, he thought—as the first time he had seen her. But she did open the door for him.

He stepped inside. The house was as he remembered it,

as overdone and pretentious as the people who lived here. Emmaline—he had stopped thinking of her as Linny some time in the past minute or so—led him into the parlor. She did not offer him a seat.

Longarm almost smiled when he saw the Logan guests. There were three gentlemen seated in the parlor. Mrs. Logan was not in evidence.

Longarm had never met Mr. Logan—hadn't heard the man's first name, either, that he recalled—but he recognized him as the least well dressed of the three. He had seen him on the street in Peyton before.

The other two gentlemen—and in their case the word applied in all of its several meanings—were very obviously strangers to this small plains town.

The two were turned out to the nines, with spats, cravats, and gaudy diamond stickpins. The older of them had a malacca walking stick at his side. The ornate knob of the cane, heavy silver studded with gems, would have fed a family of four through more than one winter. The younger would have been handsome except for the pinched, haughty expression on his highborn features.

Both men had the look of old money and inbreeding. Their glance in his direction, taking in at once his tweeds and travel-scuffed boots and much-worn revolver grips, let Longarm know how a bug must feel when a member of the superior human race deigned to look at it.

Emmaline seemed to be glorying in their company. Every move she made was a pose and a posture. She practically sparkled with a gaiety that Longarm thought was strained and false. But maybe these two dandies were so used to that crap that they thought it was normal.

"Pa*pa*," the girl said, emphasizing the second syllable the way Longarm had heard phony-French whores do, "the gentleman is a deputy United States marshal who wishes to speak with you." The words sounded stilted and syrupy to Longarm, but no one else in the room seemed to have that reaction.

Emmaline did not offer to make any introductions to the guests.

Longarm deliberately twitted the girl by laying on a po'-boy country act. He decided that p'shaw and shucks would be a bit much, but he did give the men a big grin and strode forward to tower over the older of the two dudes.

He shoved a hand forward and, in his best imitation of a deep-Texas drawl, rolled out, "You mus' be li'l Linny's daddy, suh, an' I am Custis Long o' the Yew-nited States mah-shal's office, district o' Denver. A pleasuh to make yo' acquaintance, suh."

The man looked momentarily startled. His head drew back to the full extent of his scrawny neck, as if he could gain some measure of separation from the strange creature now confronting him. It had the effect of allowing him to look down his nose at Longarm, even though the deputy stood looming far above his seated height. "You err, sir. I am A. Howard Anthony. Of the Boston Anthonys." He acted like that was supposed to mean something to Longarm. It didn't. And Longarm would not for anything have admitted to it even if the name had meant something to him.

"Reckon it's mah pleasuh anyhow, Howie," Longarm drawled. He did not really know why he was putting the old fossil on, but he damn well felt like it.

He turned to the younger man. "An' you, suh?"

The younger dude turned his head slightly to the side, quite pointedly ignoring Longarm.

It was the older man who spoke. "My son, sir. A. Howard Anthony the Fourth."

160

Longarm favored them both with a broad fool's grin. "Then you would be knowed as Howard, suh, an' this fine-lookin' young gennelmun as young Howie?"

The old gentleman sighed and gave up. "As you wish, sir." He too turned his head slightly away, as his son had just done.

Logan came to their rescue. He stood and crossed the room to take Longarm's elbow and lead him out of the room and onto the front porch. "I'm Hank Logan," he said.

He managed to ease Longarm away from the dudes with a pleasant, natural manner.

When they were outside, Longarm was amazed to see a twinkle of amusement in Hank Logan's eyes. The man had known good and well what kind of act Longarm was putting on back there. But what really surprised Longarm was his tolerant, almost pleased attitude about it. Longarm dropped the drawl.

"Sorry to have dropped in on you like that, Mr. Logan, but Race Glesson asked me to call. He'd like to borrow your buggy tomorrow so he can ride with me on an investigation he's helping me handle."

"Anything I can do for young Race," Logan said. "Use the buggy as long as you wish."

"Thank you, sir."

"Sure." Logan started to turn away, then he paused. "I hope you haven't been getting a poor impression of our town lately, Marshal. Longarm, isn't it?"

Longarm nodded. Again he had been surprised by Hank Logan.

The man smiled. "Jacob Faust is a dear friend of mine. It might help you to understand that we have very high hopes for the future of our community. And my business interests require me to deal with people of all kinds." He sighed. "Frankly, Longarm, I'd hoped that my Linny would be closer to young Race. A fine boy, that one. But fathers seldom have as much to say about their children's tastes and desires as they might wish." He sighed. "My fault, probably, for being away on business so damn much. But what the hell am I telling you all this for? Just that Jacob likes you and so does Race, I hear, and I trust their judgement. Anyway, the buggy's yours for as long as you want to use it. It's in the shed out back." That sparkle of amusement was in the man's eyes again. "Linny and her ma would probably tell you it's a carriage house, but the damn thing's a shed. Anyway, take it whenever you like. Bring it back when you're done."

"Thank you, Hank. And I hope I haven't upset any applecarts for you."

Logan grinned. "Hell, you haven't done anything to any of my applecarts. If you went and turned over one of Linny's, man, I'll consider that I owe you a drink."

Longarm laughed. "Let me know about that."

Hank Logan grinned. He squared his shoulders and said, "Once again into the lion's den."

"Goodbye, Hank."

Logan went back inside the house and Longarm headed back toward Mrs. Rurick's boardinghouse. There would be plenty of time in the morning to collect the buggy from Hank Logan's shed.

And tonight, he suspected, he could look forward to a good night's sleep. He rather doubted that he would be having a visitor this evening.

Chapter 21

The tapping at the door was so light that Longarm could barely hear it, yet it had been enough to bring him out of a deep sleep.

He got out of bed and, Colt in hand, felt his way to the locked door. "Yes?" He was standing well to the side of the door, on the off chance that someone might try to shoot him through it. Just because Curtis Bright was locked up in Denver did not mean the Watson family had run out of funds to hire a second gunman.

"Open up." The whispered voice was female. He thought it sounded like Linny Logan. That, of course, was impossible. But who...? The best way to find out would be to open the door.

He slid the bolt back and peered through a narrow opening. No sense swinging the thing wide until he knew who was out there and what she—or they—wanted.

Damnation, he thought. The lamp at the far end of the hall showed that it was indeed Linny Logan who stood there impatiently looking in both directions lest she be discovered here.

"You took your time about it," she complained in a rasping whisper as she barged inside. She stopped in the center of the room and turned with her hands planted on her shapely hips. "Well? Are you going to close that door or not?"

Longarm shook his head. Damned if he'd ever understand the female of the species. He shut the door, as ordered, and locked it again. He heard the scrape of a match, and Linny lighted the lamp.

She turned to him. "Do you always sleep in those awful things?" He was wearing his balbriggans. They probably did look pretty awful, he realized.

He grinned at her. "I thought you knew by now that I don't. Not always."

She smiled. "That's better. Do me." She turned and offered him her back, one hand lifting her blonde hair out of the way so he could reach the topmost buttons.

Obediently, Longarm began to undo the tiny buttons.

"I would quite cheerfully have scratched your eyes out this afternoon, you know," Linny said over her shoulder. "Such gall. And *such* a terrible accent. Really, Custis. That was uncalled for. Entirely uncalled for."

"You did look kinda annoyed," Longarm said.

"Of course I was. Completely."

"I really didn't expect you tonight."

Linny turned enough to give him an amused look out of the corners of her pretty eyes. "Really, Custis, you are such a *child* sometimes. One thing has absolutely *nothing* to do with the other."

"I didn't know that."

"Obviously." He finished the unbuttoning to waist level, and she slipped the gown—it was a different garment from the one she had worn earlier, but just as fancy—from her shoulders. She was not wearing anything under the dress, and the soft, molded contour of her bare back was, he admitted, damned enticing.

She turned to face him, smiled, and kissed him lightly on the lips, her dress bunched at her waist. He could feel the heat of her breasts pressing against his chest through the thin fabric of his balbriggans. "Move." She stepped out of the dress and tossed it aside, then sat on the edge of the bed to begin peeling her stockings off. She had already kicked off her unbuttoned shoes.

"I got the impression you had something going there with A. Howard Anthony the Fourth," Longarm said.

Linny favored him with a delicious smile. "And so I do," she said.

"But . . ."

"Dear, dear, Custis. I *told* you. One thing has nothing to do with the other. Howie—he hates that name, by the way, but it seemed *so* appropriate when you gave it to him; I simply cannot help myself now, and *insist* on thinking of him as Howie—is the perfect candidate for marriage. He is already quite smitten with me, poor thing. He is making hints to his father that he might wish to remain here even after their business in concluded. Perfectly obvious, of course, that he wants to pay court to me." She looked quite satisfied by that prospect.

She bent and examined what might have been a small bruise on the inside of a creamy satin thigh. Longarm was surprised only that she was not bruised further. Linny Logan was one hell of an energetic girl when she got going. She licked a fingertip with her delicate pink tongue and rubbed the spit into the blemish. It did not rub off, and she shrugged, accepting it as a mark that would soon enough go away.

"Naturally," she went on as if there had been no interruption, "I shall allow Howie to ply his suit." She cocked her head and thought for a moment. "Is that the right wording? Anyway, when a suitable amount of time and passionate embraces have passed, dear Howie will undoubtedly become so bold as to touch my bosom." She giggled. She cradled the objects in question in her palms and held them up for both of them to admire. "They aren't such bad tits, really. Are they?" She paused. "Well, are they?"

"Decent," Longarm assured her.

"Thank you. Or he may—I doubt it, but it is remotely possible—he just may choose to grab my pussy. Depends on how worked up I can get him by then. Regardless, Custis dear, once dear Howie gropes me for the first time, he is mine forever."

"Sounds thrilling." Longarm reached for the bottle of Maryland rye that sat on the bureau, uncorked it, and took a swallow.

Absently, still examining one perfect breast, Linny reached out to take the bottle from him and helped herself to a snort. She handed it back.

"It *is* thrilling. Truly. Have you any *idea* of the Anthonys' position in the Social Register, Custis?"

"No, I expect I don't." He took another swallow of the rye. It felt warm and nice as it bottomed out in his stomach. He was sure—well, pretty sure—that he was awake and not dreaming this conversation. He felt like that question kind of ought to be in doubt. "Which is more important, Linny? The money or the social position?"

She shrugged. "I don't believe I have ever tried to separate them. In fact, I don't know that that would be possible."

"You intend to marry Howie?"

She smiled. "Oh, yes."

"But you came here tonight."

She laughed. "Darling, *you* aren't going to tell Howie. I know you won't. And you are *such* a good fuck. Lord only knows how long I'll be able to enjoy my little pleasures before Howie asks me to marry him. And I *do* intend to make him a true and faithful wife, you know."

Longarm hadn't known, and still didn't believe it, as a matter of fact. "Is that in your rules, Linny?"

"Yes. Absolutely." She smiled. "Not just my rules either, dear. One never, *ever* gives that kind of ammunition to a gentleman's attorneys."

"I see." He almost thought that he did, too. He took another swallow of the rye. Linny was rising now, posturing and primping in that sensuous, sexy way she had. She moved toward him. Somehow Longarm was reminded of the smooth, slithering glide of a lazily hunting snake as it approached a plump, furry mouse it intended to swallow.

"I like your father," he said.

Linny smiled. "He likes you too." She stopped for a moment. She looked faintly puzzled. "I can't imagine why." She came to him and her arms slid—slithered?—around his neck. Her breasts, full and firm and globular, pressed against him; her pelvis rubbed hungrily at his erection.

"I ought to throw you the hell out of here," he said.

"Of course you should, dear." Hips still grinding slowly, Linny undid the buttons down the front of his balbriggans. She peeled the garment off and dropped it to the floor around his ankles.

"Mmmm." She looked down and licked her lips. With

soft laughter she dropped to her knees at his feet and began to kiss and lick his shaft from one end to the other while her fingertips played lightly with his balls. She paused. "Are you going to throw me out, Custis?"

"I don't know," he said honestly. In one way he wanted to. Emmaline Logan was not a nice person. And the acts she wanted to perform in lusty abandon with him would not be a sharing but a taking. They would mean nothing to her beyond the immediate sensation.

Yet, damn it, throwing her out of the room would be an empty gesture. It would teach neither of them, if only because he had already learned the things a man needs to know, and because Linny would never learn the things a woman should understand—things about decency and joy and giving. Those things neither Custis Long nor any other man would ever be able to teach her.

The only thing throwing her out would accomplish would be to make him go to bed with a painful hard-on. Because, like it or not, Linny Logan was as provocatively exciting as she was amoral.

Not immoral, he realized; without moral consciousness.

In a way, he felt sorry for her. He felt sorrier for Hank Logan, who had raised her, and for Race Glesson, who loved but would never possess her.

He was also, he realized, angry. Angry with Linny. Angry with himself for not refusing her.

No, he realized, he was not going to throw the bitch out. Not before he had spent himself in that glorious body, he wasn't.

Rough now, in a manner that was most unlike himself, he grabbed the hair at the back of her head and forced her forward until her nose was jammed against the mat of curling brown hair on his lower gut and her throat was filled. He felt her gag but held her there, and after a moment she relaxed and accepted all of him into her. She pressed forward even harder against him, seeking more of him. When he finally released her, her pretty face had a look of beatific happiness.

"I love for you to be rough with me, Custis. Use your belt now. Here. While I'm kneeling on the floor. Do you want me to suck your toes while you whip me? Do you?" She looked and sounded eager for any punishment or humiliation he wished to give her.

In disgust, Longarm turned and walked to the bed.

Linny followed him.

And he honestly did not know if he would turn her away this time or if he would allow her to join him there.

Linny followed. On her knees. Mouth already open. Reaching for him.

Longarm closed his eyes and shook his head. *Damn!*

Chapter 22

The buggy rolled past the empty, forlorn-looking Blake homestead. Longarm was driving. He stopped on the slope above the dugout and pointed. "That's where I buried her, Race. Beside her husband."

Glesson nodded. "They hadn't any kin that I know about. And prob'ly by now anything they had of value has been carried off."

"There wasn't anything worth shipping. You couldn't have gotten ten dollars for all of it at an auction."

"What about that well?"

"I turned the mill off before I left and dumped the tank. Best thing to do would be for you to send somebody out and have the shaft pulled, fill it in. There's no telling what they used in it. The stuff could last for years as far as I'd know."

"I'll take care of it," Race said.

They drove on. Two hours later they reached the Three Bar Seven headquarters. It was already past dinner time. They had gotten a later start than Longarm wanted, mostly because Mrs. Glesson insisted on seeing that her son was fed before he left, that the pillow wedged under his leg was just the right pillow, and that they had a lunch along fit to feed a platoon of infantry. They had had to wait half an hour while she finished frying up a tin bucket of chicken for them to carry.

Longarm waited patiently while Race fumed about his mother's motherliness.

"It's okay," Longarm eventually had to assure him. "No harm done, and the chicken will taste mighty good."

"You'd think we were going on a damn picnic instead of a murder investigation," Race grumbled.

"It's okay," Longarm repeated.

And it had been. He felt no sense of urgency. Not now. And the chicken had indeed been good. They had eaten it while they drove and tossed the bones aside for the mice to gnaw on.

They reached the Three Bar Seven, and Race asked, "What are we stopping here for?"

"You'll see."

As before, the ranch yard was empty of hands at this midday hour, but there was smoke coming from the cook-house.

There was a surrey parked in front of the main house, its pair of hired grays dozing in the sun. Longarm remembered having seen them at the livery in Peyton.

"Walker has company," Race observed.

"Uh-huh." Longarm drove on past the house and pulled the Logan buggy to a halt beside the cookhouse.

"You can't be hungry," Race said.

171

"Nope," Longarm agreed. "Couldn't eat another bite."

He climbed down the iron buggy steps to the ground and walked around to the woodpile beside the cookhouse.

"What the hell are you doing?"

Longarm grinned at him.

He bent and sorted through the sticks and twigs and bits of scrap lumber that had been thrown into a separate kindling pile beside the woodpile. Race watched while he went through the whole stack of kindling, sorting the bits into two new piles. One was an assortment of trash, the other uniform lengths of milled lumber with pointed ends and white-painted tips.

When he was done, Longarm picked up the painted pieces and carried them to the buggy. He put them under the seat.

Race bent forward and picked one up. "Looks like a stake," he said.

"So it is." Longarm climbed back into the buggy and backed the team so he could turn them away from the cookhouse.

The cook, a burly man wearing a greasy apron and a scowl, came outside. "What the fuck are you doin' here? Stealing wood?" He stalked toward the buggy. "If you think I don't see what you got under that seat...Oh, Race, I didn't recognize you right off. What's goin' on here?"

"Official business, Otis. I think you'd best go back inside and mind your own fires now."

The anger that had been in Otis's face dissolved. He wiped his hands on the already dirty apron. After a moment's hesitation he turned and went quietly back into the cookhouse.

Once again Longarm had the thought that Race Glesson was a pretty damned good local lawman. People knew him; they didn't argue with him. That was not nearly as common as it should have been.

"Nicely done, Deputy," Longarm said.

Race shrugged. "Otis and me get along pretty good now. He used to get likkered up sometimes. Liked to think he was pretty hard to take in. I guess he'd got used to bufalloing old Ed, who used to be the deputy out this end of the county. After a couple of times we worked it out. Now when I tell Otis it's time for him to come cool off, he mostly does it."

Longarm grinned. There had been no brag in that, just fact.

And, now that he thought about it, he was glad there could never be a chance for Race Glesson to get together with Miss Emmaline Logan. He liked Race too much to wish that future on him.

Longarm clucked to the team and guided them in a tight circle. He headed them back the way they had come and stopped this time beside the surrey parked in front of the house.

"Let's go in," he said.

He went around and helped Race carefully down out of the wagon, and handed him his crutches. Together, moving at Race's slow pace, they went up the gravel walkway to the front door. Longarm knocked.

"What is it?" Walker looked as belligerent as he had before. "I'm busy now, and you know already that you can't talk to any of my hands until they come in tonight."

"Yes, sir, but it's you we wanted to have a word with," Longarm said politely.

"I told you, I'm busy now."

"This won't wait, Mr. Walker. Official business."

"Please," Race added.

Walker grumbled and muttered, but he opened the door wide and let them in.

There was no parlor in the ranch house. The front room was set up as a study instead, dark and massive and masculine. Mounted elk and mule deer and bighorn sheep heads hung on the walls along with buffalo skulls and bleached longhorn spreads.

The rolltop desk was huge. A gun rack with glass doors took up most of the back wall.

The desk was open. It and a pull-out writing surface were covered with papers and ledger books.

Longarm nodded to the two men who sat in a pair of chairs fashioned from steer horns and leather. The men did not look comfortable even though they had nearly full glasses of an amber liquid at their elbows.

"Howard," Longarm acknowledged. "Howie." The older Anthony ignored him. The younger one glared.

"You know these gentlemen?" Walker asked. He did not sound especially happy about it.

Longarm smiled. "We met yesterday. But I didn't know then what their business here is."

"Their business, mister, and mine, is none of yours," Walker said.

Longarm shrugged.

Race swung on his crutches to the nearest vacant chair and turned. "I hope you don't mind, Bonny, but I've got to sit down here for a minute."

Walker grunted. It might have been permission.

"Perhaps we should return tomorrow," A. Howard Anthony the Third said, rising. "When you have more time."

"Please, I . . ."

"Mr. Walker is going to have plenty of time," Longarm interrupted. "But, come to think of it, if you do delay a little, why, I think you might find his terms more favorable than he intended."

The reference to more favorable terms apparently piqued the old gentleman's interest. He sat back down and motioned

Howie the Fourth to do the same.

"Listen, damn it," Walker blustered, "I don't care what kind of badge you're carrying; you can't come in here and shove your nose into my business."

"I wouldn't think of it," Longarm said. "What I came here for is strictly in my line of business."

"State it and get out, then."

"All right, sir. You are under arrest."

Walker's face turned red.

"For the murders of four employees of the government of the United States of America," Longarm went on.

"And," Race added, "for the murders of Murray Blake and his widow, Ida Blake."

"You are out of your minds. Both of you. You have no..." He shut up.

"No proof?" Longarm finished the sentence for him. "Wrong."

"Not completely wrong, of course," Race said. "We don't have the physical evidence we need to hang you on the Blake murders. But Deputy Long was thoughtful enough to get a search warrant while he was in Denver. It's a federal warrant, so it's good down here, in case you're wondering. We expect when we search the premises we'll come up with some kind of rat bait or coyote poison. And when we pull the casing of the Blake well we ought to find a match for whatever you use around here."

"As for the murders of the survey-crew members, we already have physical evidence to support that."

Walker's mouth was working, but nothing was coming out.

"It's funny," Longarm said, "how a man can get so used to the idea of not wasting wood in a country where there isn't hardly any wood, that he just drags it all home with

175

him. Even when that habit can connect him with a murder."

Longarm pulled a cheroot out and lighted it. He used his left hand. His right thumb was hooked casually into his gunbelt, very close to the butt of the Colt.

"Those survey stakes were going to cost you an awful lot, weren't they?" He nodded toward the Anthonys. "Those gentlemen, or someone like them, expected to buy a pretty good-sized spread out here. But those damn homesteaders like the Blakes were already making it smaller. And then damned if you didn't find out that your leases weren't near as big as they were supposed to be, either."

"Not as large as indicated, Marshal?" It was Anthony the Third who asked the question. Walker still seemed unable to speak.

"Keep an eye on our friend here, Race." To Anthony he said, "Not nearly. Walker has been running cattle on quite a spread under the old leases. I saw the maps when I was in the BLM office in Denver a couple of days ago. But I also read those maps. They're worded so that the lease conforms with rights to a certain watershed. The Three Bar Seven's leased land was supposed to be in the Arkansas River drainage. All of it. But at least half of the leased land is actually in the Platte River drainage. Hell, you can ride over that country and it *looks* like it slopes to the south. The truth is that it drains north, into the South Platte. That puts the northern half of Walker's leased land into the lease of a man up in Elbert County named Doyle. Nobody would have known anything about it until those boys from the survey crew came in here. They were mapping the divide and placing stakes along it too, working about seven miles south of where everybody, the BLM included, thought the divide was supposed to be."

He turned to Walker and said, "By the way, your boys

didn't pull all those stakes. They only pulled them up for about ten miles. I stopped off at Monument on my way back down here from Denver and rode the line out from that end. The stakes the boys planted are identical to the ones I saw in your woodpile when I was here before. When Race and I checked the murder scene we found the holes where the stakes had been, but we didn't make the connection then. When I talked to the fellows in the BLM office they told me the job was supposed to be staked. Of course, by then I already knew what the deal was down here."

Longarm shook his head. "You stupid son of a bitch, you didn't have to kill those boys. You got all panicked about losing some of the money you expected from this sale and you never stopped to think that maybe the BLM just didn't give a shit about how those leases were written. They'd just as easy rewritten the land descriptions to include ground in the Platte drainage if you'd gone to them and told them about the mistake. They didn't give a damn how it was described, and the lease could have stayed with you if you'd bothered to be honest about it. But you got all panicked and went to shooting instead. Now, mister, I reckon you're in for it."

"I . . ." Walker too shook his head.

"You're under arrest, Walker. If you want to make it easier on yourself you can surrender your pistol and let us put the cuffs on you."

Walker nodded. He stood mutely while Longarm relieved him of the revolver at his belt and clamped the handcuffs on his wrists.

"It might make things a little lighter on you if you tell us which of your people helped you," Longarm said.

Walker nodded. He looked like a beaten man. "Kestle. He's the only one. He's been with me a long time."

Longarm nodded. The name was no surprise. The two of them could have handled it alone. "Are those the guns over there?"

Walker nodded. He seemed completely compliant now that the worst had happened, quite a contrast with Curtis Bright's prison-trained reluctance.

Longarm went to the gun cabinet and opened the doors. The rack held firearms that were a hunter's dream collection, everything from saddle carbines and Sharps buffalo rifles to a Creedmore quality match rifle with sights that weighed as much as most rifles did. At one end of the rack were the shotguns. Two of those were ten-gauge fowlers. Longarm took them down from the rack and slung them across his left arm.

"I expect we're ready now, Race. If you would excuse us, gentlemen?"

The elder Anthony nodded. The younger one was still ignoring him.

With Race going first on his crutches and Bonneville Walker between them, they filed out the front door.

Chapter 23

Race was barely beyond the door and Walker still standing in the frame when both men stopped short.

"What . . . ?" Longarm heard a man's voice bark, "Shit!" and the sound of a gunshot.

Race's right hand was engaged with the crutch he had to depend on. He threw the crutch aside and grabbed for his revolver.

By then Longarm was through the doorway, knocking Walker forward, sprawling into the back of Race Glesson's wounded leg as he fell and sending Race tumbling as well.

The man in front of the house had had time to get another shot off. The slug whistled through the doorway as Longarm flung himself out and to the side. The bullet barely missed him, but it did miss, as much by dumb luck as by design.

Longarm dropped onto the floor of the porch and rolled to his right, away from the tangle of cursing bodies where Race and Walker had collided.

He rolled and stopped belly down, the Colt in his hand and pointing.

But now he had no target. The gunman had jumped back and taken shelter behind the wagon the Anthonys rented for the drive out from town.

Longarm still had not had an opportunity to get a look at the man. He had no idea who it was.

"Are you all right, Race?"

"Uh-huh." Favoring his injured leg, Race was crawling back inside the house. He was dragging Bonneville Walker by the coat collar. Walker was not impeding the young deputy's progress. Far from it, in fact. The old rancher was as eager as Race to get the hell out of the line of fire and was scrambling for all he was worth on manacled hands and busy knees.

This was hardly the time for levity, but Longarm smiled briefly at the sight of the two of them trying to crawl out of the way. Walker was half dragging Race along like a dog hitched to a sled.

"Did you see who it is, Race?"

"Kestle." The answer came from within the house.

"What the hell is he doing here at this time of day?"

There was no answer. Probably Walker did not know, either. For some reason the man had come in earlier than usual, in time to see his boss being led out of the house in handcuffs.

The reason for the arrest must have been obvious.

"Keep Walker in there with you, okay?"

"Oh, I can handle him all right." Longarm could hear the faint sound of a chuckle coming from inside the house and Race added, "Do you want me to enlist the dudes to help you out there?"

"I ain't proud. I'll take all the help I can get."

The muzzle of a revolver and then the hand that held it appeared at the back end of the surrey.

Longarm fired. He did not hit Kestle, but he damn sure made the man jump. Splinters from the painted and polished surrey flew into the air, and Longarm wondered what the livery man was going to say when the Anthonys brought the rig back. The hand and pistol disappeared with a magician's speed.

There was a row of low plantings and a two-rail fence of split saplings along the front of the yard, and Longarm cursed the man who put it there. If not for that he would have been able to see Kestle's legs under the surrey. More to the point, he would have been able to bring the man down with a bullet. There aren't too many men who will continue a fight when they have a .44 slug in the shin.

"Kestle!" Longarm called.

"Yeah?"

"There's no point to this, you know. Easier for everybody if you give yourself up."

"Fuck off."

Well, it had been worth a try. Longarm rose to his knees, then stood upright. He still could not see Kestle.

Damn!

Somehow, probably by crawling low in front of that screening brush, the son of a bitch had gotten out from behind the surrey and around to the side of the house.

Longarm barely caught a hint of motion out of the corner of his eye. He whirled, dropping into a crouch as he turned, and Kestle's bullet cut the air above Longarm's Stetson.

The double-action Colt answered, and then again.

Kestle's frame jerked with each impact, but he refused to quit. He seemed to be having some difficulty making his muscles respond the way he wanted them to, but somehow he managed once again to thumb back the hammer of his Remington revolver.

Longarm took a step forward and fired. Kestle flinched as another heavy slug slammed into his torso, and the Remington discharged into the porch flooring.

"Drop it, man. Please. I don't want to kill you."

Kestle shook his head. His face was a mask of grim determination. He held the Remington in his right hand and had to use his left to drag the hammer back for another shot.

"Damn it, man."

Kestle got the revolver cocked. He raised it, wobbly but at close range, trying to line the barrel up on his enemy.

Regretfully, but certainly not feeling hesitant or squeamish about it, Longarm thumbed back the hammer of his Colt to give him a lighter trigger pull. He took aim and finally dropped Kestle with an aimed shot to the forehead.

He discovered that he was breathing heavily even though he did not have the excuse of great exertion.

"Damn," he muttered again.

"Are you all right, Longarm?"

"Yeah, Race. I'm just fine." He reloaded the Colt and shoved it back into the holster.

Race's right crutch had been broken, either by Kestle's first bullet or as a result of the sudden and violent movements that followed. Whatever the cause, Longarm first had to handcuff Walker to the frame of Hank Logan's buggy and then help Race out and into the rig.

There was no room in the small buggy to carry Kestle's body into town, so he loaded that into the Anthonys' rented surrey, an accommodation they did not offer and about which they complained bitterly. Longarm pointed out that he could, if they preferred, commandeer the use of the surrey and send another rig out from town to collect them in a day or two. After that the dude father and dude son shut up and went along with the deputy's instructions.

The Three Bar Seven cook, Longarm noticed, had not yet made an appearance to find out what all the shooting had been about. Either the fellow had no scrap of curiosity in his makeup, or else when Race Glesson put the fear in a man he did it proper.

They rolled out of the yard and were on their way back to Peyton before any of the other hands showed up. It should be an interesting conversation around the Three Bar Seven table this evening, Longarm thought.

He felt tired but satisfied, though, even though the hard part of the job—the damned paperwork and reporting and trial preparation and testimony—was only beginning.

He rode back to Peyton that evening and well into the night listening to Race's plans to win Emmaline Logan's heart.

Assuming, Longarm thought, that she had one. But he did not say anything like that to Race. He listened without comment and hoped that the Anthonys, following in the surrey, could not hear any of that particular conversation.

With luck, Race would lose Linny, and Emmaline would win A. Howard Anthony the Fourth. Longarm was convinced that would make Race happier in the long run. But that was not the sort of thing a man could tell a friend. So Longarm rode back in silence in the company of one man who wanted Linny's hand and another man who would probably have it, and he wondered as he rode whether he would have a visitor in his room again tonight.

Probably would, he decided.

He also wondered whether he favored that probability or not. That was the hardest question of all. He still hadn't worked it out by the time they pulled into the dark streets of Peyton.

Watch for

LONGARM AND THE BLIND MAN'S VENGEANCE

seventy-second novel in the bold
LONGARM series from Jove

coming in December!

LONGARM

Explore the exciting Old West with one of the men who made it wild!

___07522-1	LONGARM AND THE EASTERN DUDES #49	$2.50
___07854-9	LONGARM IN THE BIG BEND #50	$2.50
___07523-X	LONGARM AND THE SNAKE DANCERS #51	$2.50
___07722-4	LONGARM ON THE GREAT DIVIDE #52	$2.50
___08101-9	LONGARM AND THE BUCKSKIN ROGUE #53	$2.50
___07723-2	LONGARM AND THE CALICO KID #54	$2.50
___07861-1	LONGARM AND THE FRENCH ACTRESS #55	$2.50
___08099-3	LONGARM AND THE OUTLAW LAWMAN #56	$2.50
___07859-X	LONGARM AND THE BOUNTY HUNTERS #57	$2.50
___07858-1	LONGARM IN NO MAN'S LAND #58	$2.50
___07886-7	LONGARM AND THE BIG OUTFIT #59	$2.50
___06261-8	LONGARM AND SANTA ANNA'S GOLD #60	$2.50
___06262-6	LONGARM AND THE CUSTER COUNTY WAR #61	$2.50
___08161-2	LONGARM IN VIRGINIA CITY #62	$2.50
___06264-2	LONGARM AND THE JAMES COUNTY WAR #63	$2.50
___06265-0	LONGARM AND THE CATTLE BARON #64	$2.50
___06266-9	LONGARM AND THE STEER SWINDLER #65	$2.50
___06267-7	LONGARM AND THE HANGMAN'S NOOSE #66	$2.50
___06268-5	LONGARM AND THE OMAHA TINHORNS #67	$2.50
___06269-3	LONGARM AND THE DESERT DUCHESS #68	$2.50
___06270-7	LONGARM AND THE PAINTED DESERT #69	$2.50
___06271-5	LONGARM ON THE OGALLALA TRAIL #70	$2.50
___07915-4	LONGARM ON THE ARKANSAS DIVIDE #71	$2.50

Prices may be slightly higher in Canada.

Available at your local bookstore or return this form to:

JOVE
Book Mailing Service
P.O. Box 690, Rockville Centre, NY 11571

Please send me the titles checked above. I enclose _____. Include 75¢ for postage and handling if one book is ordered; 25¢ per book for two or more not to exceed $1.75. California, Illinois, New York and Tennessee residents please add sales tax.

NAME_____

ADDRESS_____

CITY_____STATE/ZIP_____

(allow six weeks for delivery)   6